ALL TIED UP

AN ESTELA NOGALES MYSTERY

CHERIE O'BOYLE

****

O'Boyle, Cherie
        All Tied Up/ written by Cherie O'Boyle
        ISBN 978-0-997-2028-9-2

2019, Cover by Karen A. Phillips, www.PhillipsCovers.com

The complete *Estela Nogales Mystery* series:

Back for Seconds (2017) short story
Fire at Will's (2014)
Iced Tee (2015)
Missing Mom (2016)
Deadly Disguise (2017)
The Boy Who Bought It (2018)
All Tied Up (2019)

Other fiction by Cherie O'Boyle

On Scent (2019)
Not a Clue (2016) short story
An Unexpected Departure (unpublished)

Dedication
All Tied Up is dedicated to my dear friend Kathleen McCoy with eternal thanks for her encouragement and support. Keep the kettle warm up there, Kathleen, we'll join you soon enough.

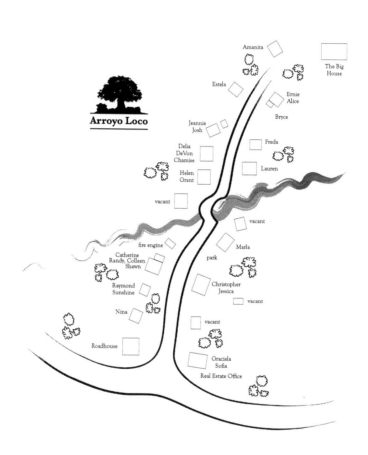

Arroyo Loco

Amanita

The Big House

Estela

Ernie
Alice

Bryce

Jeannie
Josh

Freda

Delia
DeVon
Chamise

Lauren

Helen
Grant

vacant

vacant

fire engine

Marla

Catherine
Randy, Colleen
Shawn

park

Raymond
Sunshine

Christopher
Jessica

vacant

Nina

vacant

Roadhouse

Graciela
Sofia

Real Estate Office

CHAPTER ONE

Afternoon shadows fell in Arroyo Loco, sending long rays of sun across the oak-studded California canyon. The chatter of songbirds settling in for the night and crows calling to one another as they returned to their roosts filled the early August evening.

Already late for our regular Wednesday potluck dinner, I decided to walk the short distance. Later our new street lamps would light the way home. Dogs, even well-behaved border collies, were not welcome at the dinner, so I secured Shiner and Scout inside my screened porch and headed off, bearing my platter of caprese empanadas with tomato, mozzarella, and basil filling. An unseen owl screeched from the oaks overhead, serenading my journey.

The low silhouette of the roadhouse came into view hugging the edge of the highway. No longer really a roadhouse, no longer serving barbecued ribs and coleslaw on the weekends, and no longer the site of loud live music, draft beer, and bikers, the place had slipped into retirement as Arroyo

Loco's community center. In addition to our potlucks, the roadhouse sheltered us for Saturday morning coffee klatches, homeowners association meetings, and also housed our cluster mailboxes on its wide front porch.

I bumped the door open with my hip and maneuvered in my platter of empanadas. Since I was free from my responsibilities as a counselor at the nearby state university for another two weeks, I'd decided to put some actual effort into my contribution to the potluck. Usually I showed up with whatever remained of a take-out order I had not already eaten on the way home, so it was high time to upgrade my game.

Besides, being of partially Mexican descent, I like to share my cultural heritage whenever possible. Of course I can't think of a world culture that doesn't feature some dish consisting of a dough pocket filled with whatever is available and fried, roasted, or baked. About the only aspect of an empanada that is exclusively Latin, I suppose, is the name.

"Well, well! If it isn't Doctor Estela Nogales gracing us with her presence for once," said Graciela Garcia as I entered. As the Arroyo Loco Homeowners Association president, Graciela felt entitled to comment on any member's behavior. And, in her opinion, I gave her plenty of opportunities to find fault. I'm sure my frequent absences from the regular potluck gatherings were among the least of my offenses in her eyes.

The buffet table was already loaded with delicious looking offerings, although I did notice someone had, yet again, gotten away with bringing a plate containing one apple, sliced thinly and arranged expansively.

The apple must have slipped past when no one was looking, because Amanita Warten now stood guard, arms

6

crossed, monitoring new arrivals. Even shorter than I, with a haircut that looked as though the barber had used a salad bowl as a guide, Amanita resembled nothing so much as a human mushroom. She used a finger to pull my top-heavy platter down to where she could get a good look.

Empanadas may contain any number of hearty fillings. As she gazed at mine, Amanita could only guess at what might be hidden within, but the half-moon shaped golden crusts did look tasty. She gave my platter a curt nod.

The dish having passed Amanita's approval, my friend Nina helped me wedge the large plate between casserole dishes and baskets of rolls and butter. Dusting her fingers together, Nina gazed appreciatively at my offering.

"Ooh, Estela!" she said, reaching for one. "Homemade empanadas!" Anything else Nina had to say was muffled by the juicy delight she had popped into her mouth. She dabbed a paper napkin daintily at a dribble threatening to drop onto her pale grey cashmere sweater.

I started to inquire into her well-being but was interrupted by a loud bang from across the room, followed by a string of curse words I may not have heard since junior high school. Attired tonight in a puffy-sleeved blue floral print dress, Helen Auroch stood holding aloft an apparently full twenty-cup coffee maker while Freda von Leising and another woman whose derriere I did not immediately recognize scrambled to reposition the legs on a flimsy and collapsing card table underneath. Lucky for all concerned, Helen is a quick-thinker, and also one of those big-boned women, and was bearing up well under the weight of the coffeemaker. How she manages to consistently sustain that feminine look with those biceps is beyond me.

A cluster of rumpled-looking men sat in folding chairs at the end of the table nearest Helen, but no one jumped to assist. The guys had finished setting up the tables and were now busy watching Graciela and her daughter Sofia wipe them down. Their contribution to the potluck had been to set up the tables. They waited now for the food to be served before they would move again.

When I turned back, Nina was waving me over to join the line of would-be diners gathering at the end of the long set of tables where plates were overdue to appear. My attempts at cheerful greetings were met by a fair amount of grumbling. Apparently the collapsing card table had not been the only delay to dinner this evening.

Other diners crowded in at the end of the serving line, plates arrived, and the line finally began to move. Progress quickly halted as those first in line slowed to survey the offerings before making their selections.

"Does this have meat in it?" was relayed along the line until the cook could be located and a response forwarded back to the inquirer.

"Are these gluten-free?" came the next question.

"I think Estela made those. Estela? Jessica wants to know if those things are gluten-free?"

"No. Those are empanadas filled with cheese, and the dough is made with wheat flour." I thought about tacking on "I'm sorry," but was glad I hadn't when the angry response came back.

"You know, you people here could be more sensitive to the special needs of others," Jessica said, punctuating her complaint with a disgusted huff.

Over the years of being alive and thus dealing with difficult people, one very useful skill I have learned is to keep my snarky replies to myself whenever possible. I happen to know that only about one percent of Caucasians are afflicted with a serious enough gluten intolerance to need to restrict their diets. And given the prodigious number of hot dog buns I have seen Jessica's boys consume, I am guessing precisely zero percent of her family suffers from gluten-intolerance.

Cooking food that meets with the approval of thirty or more people is hard enough without someone claiming a special need that doesn't exist. I, for example, try to avoid eating meat unless I know the animal was treated humanely, and if I'm being offered an animal to eat it was most likely executed in the prime of its life, automatically losing its "treated humanely" status. As a consequence, I try to avoid eating meat. At our potlucks I simply avoid dishes that might not pass my personal muster.

"There's a green salad right there, Jessica," I called. "Why don't you have that instead?"

"Yes, by all means," Freda added. "Have some of that salad without even one tomato on it. Help yourself." Freda lifted her lip in an uncharacteristically angry snarl and narrowed her eyes. The expression caused the pancake make-up on her seventy-something year-old cheek to crack.

"Freda," I whispered, surprised. "What's the problem?"

Freda pushed her lips into a thin line and grumbled her way to a spot at one of the dining tables, the flowing folds of her bright blue muumuu sweeping perilously close to the already shaky beverage table. I followed her over, balancing a plate sparsely populated with my own choices and sat beside her.

"Really, Freda, what's got your goat tonight?" I said, forgetting for a moment that because Freda is a native of Austria, many American English idioms make no sense to her at all.

Sure enough, she gave me a horrified look. "My goat? What has got my goat?" Her voice escalated to a higher pitch and her accent became more evident than usual. "I don't even have a goat! Are they stealing goats now?"

Any minute, Freda's voice was going to hit a frequency likely to shatter glass. I reached over slowly, so she would see me coming, and gently patted her shoulder. She had succeeded in attracting the attention of several others as they settled into nearby seats.

"It's just an expression, Freda. I only meant to ask why you're upset. You seem so angry. I'm concerned. What's going on?"

"Some fool swiped all of Freda's cherry tomatoes," Helen said as she plopped into the chair on my left. "Every last ripe tomato is gone."

Freda ground her teeth and shook her head in fury. The disappearance of her tomatoes had clearly gotten her goat, so to speak.

"My bee-yoo-ti-ful salad was all made. So beautiful." She sighed. "I went to the garden with my little bowl to get my tomatoes for the final touch and imagine! Every single one of them was gone!" Tears collected at the corners of her eyes.

"Probably those teenagers again," Bryce Bantam suggested, waving his fork for emphasis. Although close to thirty years old, Bryce, as usual, wore one of those striped tee shirts so popular with the grade school set, making him barely distinguishable from the teenagers he maligned. "More packages have been stolen off porches, too. It's probably the teenagers."

The nineteen houses strung along Arroyo Loco Road are built with their backs up to small canyons and open hillsides, and the only fences are in yards that are home to dogs. It would be easy for anyone to walk into the small garden behind Freda's house and take whatever they wanted. Similarly, our front and rear porches are available for anyone to peruse and take whatever they might desire from those locations. We rely on something like the honor system, plus a whole neighborhood of busybodies and snoops, to prevent crimes of opportunity. This has not always been a successful deterrent.

We were all still reeling, for example, by the discovery of black spray paint spattered across the front of Graciela's quaint cottage almost a month ago. Worse even than the disfiguring paint were the words the vandal had used. "Mexicans Go Home" had obliterated Graciela's perfect white house paint, and her petunias had been ripped from their flower box home and cruelly stomped.

The population of our village derives from a wide variety of cultural and ethnic backgrounds and is too small to permit dissension on those grounds. This is not to suggest there is any shortage of disagreements among neighbors. It's only that most disputes are based on differences of opinion rather than ethnic variations. Anyway, given that this land had been long a part of

Mexico, before the United States Army invaded and stole half of Mexico in 1848, we all know the suggestion that Mexicans should "go home" was ridiculous. In point of fact, this was our home. The Arroyo Loco neighbors had discussed this infuriating vandalism at numerous meetings and still had no idea who would have done such an ugly thing.

"What makes you so sure it was teenagers, Bryce?" I asked. "Did you see someone behind Freda's house taking tomatoes?"

"Of course not, Estela," he snapped. "I would have confronted those scamps if I'd seen them and demanded they return those vegetables."

"Tomatoes are fruits," Helen murmured. "He's very brave in hindsight isn't he?"

Bryce turned a glare in Helen's direction. She took a bite of broccoli and ignored him.

Nina had a question. "But who else except the kids would steal tomatoes, Estela?" I saw nods all around the table.

"Now wait a minute here," I said. "Those are our kids, and we have no evidence they've ever helped themselves to anything before." I had to stop there as a memory of some sodas missing from the small refrigerator on my screened porch flashed to mind. I dismissed that thought and went on. "Anyone could have walked into Freda's garden and taken those tomatoes." To this I got a few doubtful shrugs as folks loaded their forks with the next mouthful. "You know, there's an old saying that you should never attribute to malfeasance that which can as easily be explained by simple incompetence, or some equally plausible explanation." I could see I was losing my audience here.

"You mean, someone else could have stolen those tomatoes?" Nina said again.

"Why is everyone so sure they were stolen? Why would you jump to that conclusion? You know, the other morning I came out and found my new bird bath tipped over. I could have worked myself into a tizzy about some malicious person tipping over my bird bath ... "

Helen interrupted me. "You mean like Amanita, for example, who didn't want you to put a bird bath out there in the first place, right?"

Helen can always be counted on to bring the cynic's perspective to any situation, usually touched with a hint of humor. Some people complain that Helen's cynicism brings them down. My opinion is, if all it takes is a bit of humorous cynicism to bring you down, maybe you weren't all that up to begin with.

"Seriously?" Nina said, tucking an errant strand of her otherwise perfect coiffure into place. "Now Amanita's sneaking around at night tipping over bird baths?"

"I am doing no such thing!" came a cry from the other end of the table. Amanita had heard her name through the rest of the chatter at the dining tables.

"No!" I agreed. "Please let's don't start any rumors, and that's exactly my point. I could have assumed it was someone up to no good, but it turned out the bird bath had been tipped over by one of those wild boar who wander through our neighborhood now and then. Diego helped me right it, and we could see the tracks all around in the area. It's August, and it's dry. The poor boar probably just wanted a drink of water."

"So you think it was a wild boar and not the usual bore?" Helen said, tipping her head in Amanita's direction. Helen caught my disapproving scowl and leaned in close. "Before you get to feeling all sorry for Amanita, 'Stel', you know she's done plenty around Arroyo Loco to bring everyone's frustration down on her."

"Are those darned boar back?" Raymond Watts, our most senior neighbor, scowled. "I thought we had those darned things all sterilized."

"Sterilized, yes, Raymond," Helen called to his end of the table. "Not eliminated. There's still a few wandering through now and then."

Nina cut me a sideways glance. "Let me get this straight. Are you saying you think the boar may have eaten Freda's tomatoes?"

Before I could answer with my point about how that was only one of a number of possible explanations, Freda cut me off.

"*Nein, nein*, Estela." She parked a chubby fist on one hip and snarled. "I am so sure the boar carefully picked every one of my ripe tomatoes. Those boar are big, and not so clever, *ya*? The boar would have made a much bigger mess."

"Yeah, duh, Estela," Helen said in that tone that so endears her to others. "Even one boar would have torn those plants to shreds and trampled everything."

If this had been a cartoon, it would have shown steam coming out of my ears at that point. I took in several deep breaths while everyone else chuckled along with Helen about that doofus Estela.

"My point is," I said in a slow and deliberate tone, "we don't need to assume those tomatoes were stolen by anyone. Maybe the scrub jays found them and took a liking. Birds could have picked them without leaving a trace."

Our resident aging hippie psychic, and Raymond's partner, Sunshine Rainbow smiled at me from her end of the table. "Yes, Estela may be exactly correct. The universe provided perfect delicious tomatoes and sweet birds to share our bounty. Estela may very well be right." She flipped her graying braid over her shoulder and turned her beatific smile to everyone. Most were still focused on cleaning their plates. Either that, or no one was inclined to give up griping and radiate Sunshine's positive light just yet.

"What about these packages stolen off porches, then?" Bryce asked. "Birds carried those off, too, you think?" He raised his eyebrows at me, making his point. "And since when do birds use cans of spray paint?"

I glanced back at the table laden with half-empty food dishes, remembering a freshly baked apple pie sitting there somewhere between the sweet potato casserole and Freda's tomato-less salad. Slipping away from this conversation and taking a nice slice of pie home to enjoy in peace beckoned.

"And it was not a bird who moved my flowerpots, either," Nina said. "When I got home from work today I noticed someone had moved those pots." She placed two fingers over her lips, then continued. "My house key was under there, and it's gone now."

CHAPTER TWO

Nina's announcement that her spare house key had gone missing resulted in gasps all around.

"*Mein Gott*," Freda cried. "Someone has stolen your house key? You must be terrified! What ever will you do?"

It took several minutes for the story of the missing key to be repeated along the tables so that folks who had been too busy jabbering could be clued in. When shocked faces were all aimed in Nina's direction, she nodded and said, "A locksmith is coming tomorrow, of course, and I'm staying with a girlfriend in Morro Bay tonight."

"What about your stuff?" Amanita said, a look of horror darkening her face. "All your stuff could be stolen."

Raymond leaned in. "Sunshine and I already offered to watch Nina's house." He coughed deeply two or three times, and continued. "I don't sleep much anyway. We'll watch out."

"You know what we need?" Bryce had one of his bright ideas. "We need cameras. My dad could rig up videocameras on each of our porches. Plus we could put one over the park and one aimed at the entrance to the highway. As long as Nina is not going to allow us to install a gate across the road ... " Here he narrowed his eyes at Nina, who was snickering with Sofia on her other side and missed the dig. "Anyway, we could at least have a videocamera there. That way we could see who's snooping all over, spraying paint, and stealing things."

"Oh, great idea, Bryce," Helen said. "Criminy, you really want to live with videocameras watching your every move? Anyway, who even cares enough to watch all of those video recordings? Someone needs to get a life!"

Unwisely deciding to jump back into the fray, I asked, "Is that really happening here, anyone? I mean, I've seen it on television, on the news, other places, but is it really happening here? Has anyone had a package taken off their porch? We all buy things on line now. Has anyone missed a delivery?"

Mostly I got blank looks.

"I think my mom had something taken," Sofia said softly.

We turned to look at the end of the table where Graciela was absorbed in a quiet conversation with Jessica and her husband Christopher.

"Mom? Mom?" Sofia finally succeeded in gaining her mother's attention. "Dr. Nogales wants to know if you've had any packages stolen."

"Who?" Graciela asked.

"You know, Dr. Nogales," Sofia said, then resorted to pointing at me. "Estela Nogales." Her instructions in manners apparently covered the use of formal titles, but did not advise not pointing at people.

"Oh. Why?"

My turn. "Sofia said she thought you might have had a package stolen. We're just trying to find out if anyone has had anything stolen off their porch."

"Oh, well, not my porch. The real estate association sent me a gift box. Nuts and dried fruits. That kind of thing. And UPS says they left it at the front door of the real estate office. The door facing the highway, you know." She pointed vaguely off across the road in the direction of her office. "I never got it, but I just assumed some wild animal helped themselves. I don't know that another person would take it."

Nina leaned across me to make eye contact with Graciela. "That hardly counts anyway, *sí*, because that door is on the highway side?"

Our nineteen or so houses are all arranged along Arroyo Loco Road, including the Garcia's cottage and front door. To the side of Graciela's home and facing the highway is the addition she had built to house her real estate office. Usually displaying garish signage and with a barren gravel parking pad out front, we try to pretend the real estate business is not a part of our neighborhood.

"Yes, that's true," I said. "So we're back to the question." Maybe I'd get an answer this time, since I now had the attention of most of the diners. "Has anyone here ever had a package delivery stolen off their porch?"

A heartbeat of silence followed my question. Then Bryce jumped in. "No, but I saw it on television. Brazen the way they walk right up and take packages. We should install cameras."

A generally agreeable mumbling followed, probably people remembering seeing porch thefts on television, rather than to the notion of installing cameras.

Nina added another thought. "Delia's kids had a bicycle stolen from their back patio a couple years ago, remember?"

"Ooh, yes," Freda said. "And Amanita's lawn chair was stolen from in back of her house, too. Yes, Amanita?"

"Oh, good," I said, mostly under my breath. "Now we need to install cameras in the rear of our houses, too." An easy way to put the kibosh on this whole idea was to suggest that Bryce work up a budget for installing cameras. Once folks got wind of how much that would cost, the idea would die a natural death. I decided to save that for another more dire occasion. I scooted my chair back and rose. It was time to get my slice of pie and get out of there.

Just in the nick of time, too, because with a thundering across the wooden porch of the roadhouse, a small troupe of our aforementioned teenagers arrived. We have a sort of an unwritten rule at our Wednesday potlucks that after we've all served ourselves, the teenagers are permitted to sail in and consume every remaining morsel of food. That saves on having nearly as much to do in the way of clean-up, but it also means that if anyone wants seconds, they'd better get them before the kids arrive. There was a scramble on the part of the adults to snatch extra helpings and dessert, and Helen busied herself making a quick plate to take home to her new husband, Grant.

"Where is Grant?" I asked, placing my healthy slice and a half of pie on the empty empanada plate and securing it tightly in the left-over plastic wrap. "Is he sick?"

"No, no," Helen said. "Grant never gets sick. He's a horse that way. No, he had to stay late at work. Didn't you see it on the news?"

Grant works as a guard at the nearby prison, officially called a men's colony, over on Highway One. Hearing that he had to work late, and that there was something on the news about it, caught the attention of several people.

"Ooh, yes!" Freda said. "I saw that on the local report! A prisoner, he escaped, yes?"

"Not escaped, exactly," Helen said. "They were getting him ready to transfer over to the state mental hospital at Atascadero and he somehow went missing. They think he's still on the prison grounds, they're just not sure exactly where."

"Hold the phone, Helen," I said. "Why would they send a convicted felon to the state mental hospital? Is he a criminal or a nut?" I know that as a mental health professional I shouldn't be using common vernacular, particularly of a derogatory nature, but sometimes the demands of communication supersede propriety.

"A little bit of both, I suppose," Helen said. "He's criminally insane, and probably brain-damaged. Guys are transferred back and forth all the time." As a recently retired librarian at the men's colony, Helen would know.

"What sort of a criminal is he?" Nina asked, more to the point. "A murderer or what?"

"Oh, violent. Definitely a violent guy. That's why they wanted him out of the men's colony. Most of that place is really more of a country club for white collar criminals. The really bad guys go some place more secure. Anywho, the place is on lockdown while everyone searches for the guy, and Grant had to work late."

"I had no idea there was such a fine line between a violent criminal and a mentally ill person," I mumbled to no one in particular as I gathered my things.

Helen chuckled. "Oh, Estela, there's a finer line than you think between the criminally insane and the rest of us."

That's when we noticed the group of teenagers gathered near the door, listening intently. Graciela called to her daughter, who had joined her ravenous peers. "Sofia, come home with me. Hurry! Helen says there's an insane criminal on the loose."

Jessica and Christopher gathered their brood, and the whole crowd of them took off, skipping dessert and leaving a good hour earlier than usual, followed closely by several others.

"Wait just a minute, there!" Freda called. "You're not all going to leave me alone here cleaning out the coffee pot and the kitchen! And you boys there, you fold those tables and chairs, please." She said boys, but she was pointing at the men trying to slip away unnoticed. Grumbling, they returned to do as they had been ordered.

I fetched a clean damp dishrag from the kitchen and began wiping the food table as serving dishes and utensils were scooped up by their owners. By seven-thirty, Helen, Freda and I were the last ones to leave, turning out the light and locking the door behind us. Our weekly potluck had fizzled quickly.

Bryce was waiting out front in his mini-pickup to give Freda a ride to her place. Assuming Helen also had her car parked nearby, I waved goodbye to Freda and turned to Helen.

"Where's your car?"

"Oh," she said, "we sold my little Honda. We're going to sell Grant's Buick, too, and buy something newer, something we can both get into."

I may have already mentioned that Helen is a big woman, and Grant is even bigger. It was not easy to imagine him stuffing himself into Helen's tiny Honda. "Sounds like a good idea," I said. "So how are you getting home?"

"Don't you have a car here?"

"No. An important component of my fitness plan, as you well know, is to try to walk instead of driving whenever I can. My car is home in the driveway. I was hoping you would bring yours."

"Huh, Some fitness plan, hoping someone else will drive you home. I guess we're both hoofing it then. Let's go."

And with that, we started uphill in the dusk, carrying leftovers and empty dishes.

"Let's hope," Helen said, "we don't run into any tomato thieves on the way."

"That's a thought." I gazed ahead of us, widening my eyes and trying to activate what scant night-vision I might have, as a human. "What do you think happened to Freda's tomatoes?"

"Whoo-ee, 'Stel, I have no idea. It's possible, you know, she picked them herself and lost track of where she put them."

"Good point. You think she's having memory issues?"

Helen huffed, although in response to my question or just because we were making steady progress up the steep part of the hill, I couldn't say for sure. She stopped and put one hand on a hip, then shook her short blond hair. "Hard to say, 'Stel. You know we're all sort of discombobulated with what all's going on in the world. Freda might have picked those tomatoes, then gotten distracted with something else and forgotten them. Does seem like she would remember later, though, or at least remember picking them."

23

"Hmm. So maybe they really were stolen. Remember when someone was eating ice cream out of the community freezer? Maybe this is something similar."

"Yeah, might be. Might even be the same someone."

We had reached the driveway to the fire engine garage, and both turned to gaze at Marla Weisel's house across the road.

"Sort of hard to imagine Marla going to all the trouble to climb the hill and hike behind Freda's for a handful of tomatoes," Helen said. "On the other hand, the rich are getting richer and the rest of us are just hanging on. Possibly Marla, or anyone else who was hungry, helped themselves to what they saw as free food."

"Good point." We moved on, starting across our new steel bridge. "Somehow it's easier to understand the ice cream theft. I mean, that was irritating, but more easily understood. This kind of petty theft is less explicable and more irritating. Like those package thefts you see on the news. That would be really annoying to have something you'd ordered and paid for stolen. What would some total stranger do with the replacement part for my blender that I ordered last week? The ice cream thefts were upsetting, but nowadays people are evidently having blender parts swiped from their porches. That would really tick me off."

Helen considered my argument. "Or possibly these days, with everything that's going on in the world we're all more easily ticked off, irritated, and scared."

I had to agree. "Do you think someone really took Nina's key from under her flowerpot?"

"As opposed to what, 'Stel'?"

"Could have been something simple, like someone moved it to irk Nina, or maybe to scare her." Setting aside for a moment the question of why someone might want to irk or scare Nina, I said, "Maybe she moved it herself, and then forgot she did it? A month from now, she might find that key in her junk drawer, or someplace else she doesn't expect."

Helen looked down on me, chewing her lower lip. "Might be a limit to how much mischief goes on in Arroyo Loco you want to blame on forgetfulness, 'Stel'".

"You have a point there," I had to admit. "So who would want to scare Nina?"

Still gnawing on that lip, Helen shook her head. Neither of us having any answers, we continued on to her driveway.

I had just waved goodbye and continued along the sidewalk when a wide set of headlamps came across the bridge and turned into Helen's driveway. Grant, finally returning in his boat of a Buick. I hoped that meant the prison escapee had been found and returned securely to custody. I scurried homeward, toward the company of my godson Diego and his new wife Alex, my dogs, and the warmth and safety of our crowded but cozy home.

Lying awake that night, I found myself worrying about Nina's safety. Having someone unknown swipe the hidden key to her house had to have her feeling nervous, even though she wasn't staying in the house that night. I know I'd be freaking out. It had to have been someone who knew her key was under there. Who might that have been? On the other hand, I suppose, under flowerpots are fairly common places to hide house keys, and maybe the first place a would-be burglar might look.

None of my neighbors in Arroyo Loco are family to me, although after so many years here and all the adventures and arguments we've shared, sometimes it feels like they are family.

That got me started thinking about how and why I'd stayed in the settlement of Arroyo Loco. This house had been in the Nogales family as long as I could remember, passed down from ranch-hand grandfather to the next destitute cousin. When I had arrived, I'd intended to stay only a few months between jobs. The house was in bad repair when I moved in, and I'd always thought of the place as a kind of a way station, a layover, on my way somewhere else. Then somehow, I never moved on.

In fact, I thought, I've always been able to picture myself living another life. Somewhere in a parallel universe I'm living in a much nicer house with an attentive husband and maybe two kids. Of course the kids would be teenagers by now, or possibly off to college already.

Then, every morning, I wake up to being here instead, mostly alone in this ramshackle bungalow. Still, even after all these years, I think of Arroyo Loco, and my life here, as a stopover. Maybe that sense of impermanence explains why I find home repair and improvement to be so challenging. Nowadays, Diego does all the work needed to keep the place safe and habitable, and I've hardly ever done anything, save that time I tried to clean and paint the kitchen ceiling.

So it's true, I've never really felt at home here. Then again, where have I ever felt at home? I was born later in my parents' lives, after they had settled into a comfortable marriage. They never failed to assure me that I was a wanted child, but I still always felt a bit like a guest in their home. And that's what I felt like here, too. A temporary guest of the Nogales family in their forever falling apart bungalow along a winding highway in the cattle rangeland of the coastal foothills of central California.

I rolled over, punched my pillow, and tried to will my mind to stop spinning.

CHAPTER THREE

Thursday started as any ordinary morning. I was determined to get back into the rhythm of a workday schedule well before the semester began this year. I waited until the hub-bub Diego and Alex made as they traded places in the bathroom and got ready for their jobs had died down before I crawled out of bed, then joined them on the porch for coffee. Not wanting to upset them, I did not mention the missing tomatoes, and kept the conversation focused on the new planting bed they had prepared for me to the side of the driveway. They left shortly afterward, in a hurry to beat the traffic, and I had the bathroom to myself for my own ablutions. By eight o'clock, Shiner and Scout were leashed and ready for their morning walk.

We headed out and turned downhill. I strolled, taking in deep breaths of the cool, lightly skunk-scented air. The dogs enjoyed their own universe of smells in the underbrush to the right of the sidewalk. The sound of a motor came from behind us, accompanied by a rhythmic *whine-whine-whine*. I'm no expert, but it sounded like an engine problem Amanita should have checked soon. Maybe a loose fan belt. She drew even with us, rolled down her passenger window, and leaned over."

"Those dogs better be on leash, Estela. Both of them!"

I smiled and gave her a cheery wave. Really, what else was there to do? She continued on her way, leaving me with thoughts about why, with all of the ugliness going on in the world today, anyone would feel the need to pile-on. My mood darkened as I thought about how it almost seems like everyone is looking for ways to make life harder for others. Although in fairness, I realized, Amanita is pretty much always like that, so maybe gross generalizations weren't fair.

We'd made it to the front of Helen's house and were getting ready to cross the driveway when we were all startled by Grant's Buick backing out fast. He must have caught sight of us at the last minute because he slammed on his brakes, which then caused his trunk lid to fly open. A sickening crack sounded as his rear window shattered into a million small chunks. I had never seen Grant angry, and I wasn't looking forward to the experience as he threw open his door and propelled himself to the rear of his car. At first, he surveyed the damage in fuming silence, his face growing more purple by the second.

He finally spoke, his voice tightly controlled. "Why is my trunk open?"

I wasn't one hundred percent sure he was even talking to me. After all, I was essentially an innocent bystander. I lifted my shoulders in a shrug, but did not dare utter a sound. We both turned to stare into the wide open trunk, looking for an answer inside.

Helen flounced down their porch steps, dressed this early morning in a blue flowered house dress and matching scuffs. She came to join us in peering into the trunk.

Any gathering of two or more neighbors is bound to quickly draw a crowd in Arroyo Loco. A minute or so later, we were joined by Delia from next door, dressed to dash off to work and preceded by a cloud of her musky perfume. Toting a mug of morning coffee, she must have spotted us from her breakfast table.

"What on earth is the excitement about now?" Then she spotted the cracked window. "Boy, howdy!" Her eyes widened and she whistled.

"Yeah, I'll say," Helen added. "Somebody must've pried open your trunk, hon. You didn't drive home with it that way last night. It must have happened after you got home."

Grant pulled the trunk lid to eye-level and we all scanned the undamaged edge. The paint wasn't even scratched. He let the lid rise. "No one needed to pry it, anyway" he said. "I don't lock it. All they had to do was open it."

"Hmm," I said. "Do either of you sleepwalk?" Both Helen and Grant turned slowly to glare at me. "Anybody on Ambien, maybe?" The glares deepened, eyebrows lowered. "Well, someone wanted to get in there. Who else would want to get into your trunk? And look, the carpet's pulled up, and the jack and lug wrench are out."

Helen peered inside again. "Why would anyone want to steal our jack?"

"And if they got in there to steal the jack, why didn't they take it?" Delia said, "'Cause there it sits."

Grant reached across and pulled the carpet farther back, revealing the spare tire still resting in its cubby. "They weren't after the tire either."

"What else would someone have been looking for?" I said. "Helen's golf clubs are still there. Are any of those missing, Helen?"

Delia decided to answer, although how she would know if anything was missing from Helen's golf bag was a mystery to me.

"Naw ... they were looking for somethin' else in there. Somethin' serious like drugs, or money, or guns."

Grant scowled while Helen's eyebrows shot skyward. "Guns?" The pitch of her voice escalated a notch. "Drugs? What would Grant be doing with guns or drugs in his trunk?"

"I'm not sayin' he had drugs," Delia said. "I'm jus' saying someone might'a been looking for drugs. Why would someone be getting into your trunk? What else you got in there someone might'a been looking for?"

Silence reigned for a few seconds while we all considered the possibilities.

"My birthday present?" Helen said, turning to Grant. "Were you hiding my birthday present in your trunk?"

"Helen," I said, "what are you suggesting? That you went looking for your birthday present in Grant's trunk, and then left it open? Wouldn't you remember if you'd done that?"

"Not if she's on that Ambien stuff, she wouldn't have," Delia pointed out.

I stepped judiciously to the side as Helen feinted a move to pull a club out of her golf bag. The look on her face clearly said she intended to aim for Delia's head.

"Use your words," I quietly reminded Helen.

"Nobody here is on Ambien, Delia!" Helen said. "And there are no other drugs either! Would you clam up!"

Grant got ahold of Helen's arm, but his own face had turned dark again. "Any idiot can see what with the spare tire and all, there's nothing in there, not drugs, not guns, and not any birthday presents!"

"Of course not if they've been stolen already!" Delia snapped, then stepped back when confronted with the combined force of both Helen and Grant united in fury. "All right!" she yelled. "You asked the question! I'm jus' gonna get outta here before someone starts gettin' physical." With that, Delia put her hands in front of her face, palms out and backed away, bumping into Bryce who was just arriving at the scene of the excitement.

"What's going on?" Bryce asked, then said, "Whoa! What happened to your window, Grant? Bummer!"

I waited until Delia was mostly out of earshot, and didn't bother to respond to Bryce. "Yes, I think we all need to chill here. You know how we were talking last night about the mischief that's been happening in Arroyo Loco? This is probably another act of mischief. Whoever got into your trunk was probably just exploring. No harm done ... at least, no harm done until the car backed up fast and the window shattered." I didn't think there was any point in mentioning that if Grant had not reversed quite so fast, he might have noticed the trunk was unlatched before it had a chance to smash into the window. "We're all snapping at one another needlessly."

Bryce leaned inside the trunk, although since he had no background on what had happened I didn't know what he thought he might be hoping to find in there.

In forlorn contemplation of his window, Grant grumbled. "That's gonna cost a cool couple hundred to fix, at least. My deductible is five hundred, so chances are it'll cost more like four hundred and ninety-nine bucks."

The four of us stood gazing morosely into the interior of the trunk. In all likelihood, Grant was exactly right, but I still didn't see how he'd not noticed before he started off that the trunk lid was open, or at least unlatched. Don't most cars have a light on the dashboard that warns drivers when the doors are open? The repair would cost him, but the damage had to be his fault.

Then I noticed something odd. From my new position a couple of steps back, I could see a dent on a metal part of the underside of the lid and a scratch across the paint. That was a fresh scratch, too. A curly strip of paint still clung to the end of the scratch line. I stood in silence, trying to picture what might have happened there.

"What, 'Stel'?" Helen said, watching me.

"I don't know, exactly, but I don't think whoever was messing in your car was trying to steal your jack. Look." I stepped forward and pointed at the dent, which had a definite round shape to it. "It almost looks like someone was inside the trunk, using the jack to press on the underside of the trunk lid." I moved the jack over so it stood directly under the dent. The top of the jack fit perfectly into the shape of the dent.

Helen and Grant leaned in to get a better look, then both stood and looked at me in confusion.

"Here's what I think happened," I said. "I think someone was inside the trunk, maybe locked inside the trunk, and used the jack to push open the lid from the inside."

"Huh?" Bryce was confused. "Why didn't he pull the latch release and get out of the trunk that way? There's supposed to be a release mechanism here for if someone stuffs you into the trunk and you need to get out." Bryce didn't explain how he had come to know this essential fact, and I, for one, wasn't interested in that story anyway. He leaned inside again, feeling for a latch release. He didn't find one.

"Latch releases weren't required in cars made before the model year 2002," Grant explained. "This Buick was manufactured in 2000, before the law."

"Oh. So no latch release, huh?" Bryce pursed his lips and nodded solemnly. "Good to know."

I wondered how, in a case where one is about to get stuffed into a trunk, one could make certain the car in question had been manufactured after 2001. Exercising my better judgment for once, I left the question unasked.

Helen was working her way into another good fume. "Okay, 'Stel' you think someone was inside the trunk and got out by using the jack to push open the lid. And you think this might have been another one of those dad-gum pranks. Who would've gotten in there, and what on earth for?"

"Those are good questions, Helen. We've been so focused on how the trunk lid came to be open, we weren't even wondering why anyone would get in there in the first place. Grant says the car wasn't locked last night. Because anyone could have gotten in there if it was unlocked. Maybe a small child walked by, saw it was open, lifted the lid, and crawled in just, well, you how kids are. A child might have crawled inside for no particular reason at all."

Helen lowered her brow at me. "And then the child's obnoxious older brother came along and slammed the lid, trapping the poor child inside?"

Hmm. Sounded as though Helen herself may have suffered at the hands of a tormenting older brother. I was about to ask about that, when Grant jumped into the discussion.

"That's a fine story, but what kid is going to know to use the jack to get out of there?"

"Hmm. You're right about that, Grant," I said. "Once inside, no matter who it was, they wouldn't be able to get out without doing something like what they apparently did, and it is hard to imagine a child being that resourceful or knowledgable. As to why they might have gotten in there in the first place, we're still left with no ideas. I haven't the foggiest."

Another silence fell while we all considered the obvious. That prison escapee. "Is there any chance, Grant, that yesterday's escapee could have gotten inside your trunk?"

Grant's reply thundered. "Don't be ridiculous! Employees' cars are parked in a secured yard. The whole reason my darn car was unlocked is because we all had to unlock them so they could be searched on the way out the gate. Guy would have to be nuts to think he could get out of that yard in anyone's trunk. A person can smother to death inside a car trunk, you know! He'd have to be nuts!"

I let that percolate for a few seconds. First, I did not know that a person could smother inside a car trunk, and I was betting a guy attempting to make a bold escape from prison wouldn't have known that either. Second, had it not occurred to Grant that the guy was in the middle of being taken to the mental hospital? Quietly, so as to arouse as little anger as possible, I said, "Well, he was being transferred to the state hospital for the criminally insane, so, well, maybe yes on the nuts thing." I didn't get any nods to my idea.

"I'm late," Grant said, and he slammed the trunk lid closed. Or that was at least the intent. The latch must have been damaged in the process of being forced, because the lid flew open again, almost nicking Grant's head as it did. It simply was not possible for Grant to express any greater degree of anger than he already had done. He glared at me, one eye narrowed to a slit, and turned to Helen. "You got a rope or something?" He lifted Helen's golf clubs out of the trunk that could no longer be locked, and stood them at her side.

I unhooked Shiner's frayed leash and handed it to Grant. We had plenty more at home. Grant got busy trying to figure out where to loop the leash and how to tie it. Now free, Shiner wandered over and started smelling the edge of the trunk lid. He slid his snout most of the length of the opening, then moved back to focus on the area near the center. His nostrils flared and contracted, drawing in all the scent information he could gather. Sadly for us poorly equipped humans, he could not communicate the results of his careful study.

Grant got the trunk secured, climbed back into the driver's seat without so much as a smooch for his wife, and drove away. Helen, Bryce, and I stood, watching him disappear across the bridge.

"You really think that brain-damaged looney tunes escaped convict could have been in Grant's trunk?" Helen said. She gazed suspiciously at the shadows under the nearby trees.

37

"Because, you know, if he was in there, he sure as heck isn't in there any longer, so where is he now?"

That made Bryce and I also inspect the shadows and other places nearby that a man might possibly be concealed. I could feel the hairs on the back of my neck begin to rise.

"We should call an emergency HOA meeting," Bryce said. "All-hands-on-deck kind of emergency meeting."

"Really, Bryce?" I said. "Don't you think everyone will want to stay inside if there's a bad guy roaming Arroyo Loco? Folks will be too afraid to go off to a meeting, leave the kids alone at home, or go home to an empty house after the meeting."

"Anyway, what would be the point of a meeting?" Helen asked.

Bryce was frustrated. For once he was the guy in possession of the latest news, and he wanted to be the one to share it. "Yeah, okay, but we should go tell all the neighbors, at least. Tell them to keep their eyes out for him."

I shot Helen a look, which she returned. Telling the neighbors wasn't a bad idea, really. Me, personally going door to door to do the telling was not a good idea. I shook my head. "I want to go home."

Helen had an even better idea. "How about we each go home and start a phone tree. I'll call everyone with last names from A to M, and Estela, you can call everyone from N to Z."

"What should I do?" Bryce whined, unhappy with his role in this plan.

"You can go secure the roadhouse," Helen said. "Check for any damage and post a note on the door about the potential situation."

Bryce muttered, "potential situation," to himself, but remained unconvinced. "Should I say the escapee is here? Or we don't know and so everyone should keep an eye out? 'Cause, you know, it could be anybody who got into your trunk."

Grant's Buick with its busted rear window had not been gone more than five minutes before doors started opening and more neighbors began appearing. Freda swept across the road in a brilliant maroon and yellow muumuu, her orange hair and garish red lipstick already in place, and a huge green purse slung over one arm.

"Well, well, well. What has happened here? You are all gathered out here so early. What is this excitement all about?"

Happy to have someone pay attention to him at last, Bryce proceeded to explain about Grant's broken window and the mystery of who got locked in the trunk. Freda made all of the appropriate oohs and aahs, then took her leave. "Toodle-oo," she said. "I'm off to do some marketing."

"Don't forget the tomatoes," Helen called, in what I personally thought was an unnecessarily cynical bit of humor. Giving Bryce a narrow-eyed look, Helen pulled me closer. "Really, 'Stel', who do you think was in Grant's trunk?"

CHAPTER FOUR

Helen's attempt at being secretive failed.

"I can hear you, you know," Bryce said in an indignant tone. Helen faced me, eyebrows raised. "No, really, Estela, who do you think was in Grant's trunk?"

"Have I mentioned before, Helen, that a lot of people tend to get the terms psychologist and psychic mixed up, or think those two words mean the same thing? I don't know any more than you do about who might have decided to crawl inside there. The trunk was unlocked all night, so Bryce is right. It might have been anyone."

At this, Bryce puffed out his chest, stretching the stripes on his well-worn tee shirt. I always forget he's one of those guys who grows an exaggerated sense of his own self-importance with the slightest encouragement.

I gave the question some additional thought as I gazed into the distance. "I will tell you one thing, though. Whoever it was, it had to be someone who, finding themselves locked inside, had the smarts or the experience to think of using the jack to push open the lid."

"So, not one of Christopher's boys, then?" Helen said.

"I hadn't even thought of those kids. What's the oldest one, nine? Why would they leap to mind? Don't Christopher and Jessica keep a tight rein on that brood?"

Helen rolled her eyes. "Oh, you might be surprised what goes on in this part of the canyon, 'Stel'."

She was right, no doubt, but I wasn't in the mood for a neighborhood gripe session at that moment.

"I know what you mean though, Estela. The guy locked in the trunk was not a total mush-brain. He had to be someone who knew how to use tools." She cut a meaningful glance in Bryce's direction. "Like your dad, Ernie, for example."

Bryce was instantly outraged. "What? What would my dad be doing in that trunk? My dad can't even walk! Have you forgotten he's confined to a wheelchair since the accident?"

"Okay, okay, calm down. I'm only trying to think of who might be smart enough to think of getting out of the trunk by using the jack."

In an attempt to diffuse Bryce's anger, I brought the question back to what I considered the essential issue. "Figuring out who was in that trunk might be easier if we understood why someone might have gotten in there in the first place."

Helen gave me a long look. "A motive, you mean?"

I raised my shoulders and dropped them. Who knew?

Helen shook her head and moved on. "Okay, well right now, we'd better get the word out to the neighbors. It'd be a darn shame if someone got hurt because we were too busy out here jawing to get the word out. You have your mission, Bryce?"

Somewhat placated with the remark implying his dad was smart, and swelled up with his "mission," Bryce pushed off in

42

the direction of the roadhouse at a moderate speed, his skinny elbows swinging.

Helen waited until he was out of earshot, watching him go. "Dimwit," she muttered, then turned to me. "Do you remember, that day? After you got your binoculars out? Do you remember when we saw Ernie stand and walk across his porch when he thought he was alone?"

I nodded slowly. I did remember, but could not imagine what would possess Ernie to walk to Grant's Buick in the middle of the night and climb inside the trunk.

"I'll tell you what else," Helen said. "Whoever pried their way out of that trunk, they also helped themselves to my nine iron." She gestured at the clutch of golf clubs poking out of the purple bag. I wouldn't know a nine iron from a wedge at first glance, but Helen seemed convinced. "And maybe some other stuff, too." She reached into pockets and peered into pouches. "Like my gloves. I think my golf gloves are gone. Unless I left them somewhere."

I made compassionate noises.

"You know who else we should call, Estela? We should call your friend Detective Muñoz. This has gone beyond mischief. A crime has been committed here."

"Yes," I said, thinking a stolen nine iron and a missing pair of golf gloves hardly constituted a crime serious enough to warrant the attention of a sheriff's detective. "Maybe I'll do that when I get home."

"I certainly hope so. This whole thing has made me darn nervous. Okay, so you go home and make your phone calls beginning with N. Meanwhile, back at the ranch here, I'll call A through M."

Normally I wouldn't let Helen boss me like that, but since all I wanted to do was get home anyway, I saluted obediently and headed off, Scout pulling ahead on his leash and Shiner following at my heels.

Returning home, I had a moment of concern when I realized I had apparently left the house without locking any doors, although I could swear I had at least thrown that latch on the screen door. Might be time for me to revise old habits. On the other hand, my dogs could be counted on to sound a noisy alarm upon encountering any unfamiliar and unexpected smells. Neither showed any sign of an alert at that moment. Instead, they both went directly to their food bowls on the ever-present chance that a delicious morsel or two had been magically deposited there since they'd last checked.

I took a deep breath, relishing the quiet alone time. It's not that I don't adore my roommates, Diego and Alex. Without them, I don't know how I could possibly maintain this place. All the same, quiet is a treasure also.

Extracting my new Arroyo Loco phone list from the bottom of the junk drawer in the kitchen, I sank into my recliner and pulled the phone close. Let's see. My task was to call all residents of Arroyo Loco whose last names began with N through Z. I folded the sheet in half and perused the names I had been assigned.

There I was at the top of that list. Nogales. I put a big check mark by that one. Done. Next name was Raskin, Josh and Jeannie. New to the neighborhood, but they seemed like nice enough people. I reached to dial, then realized the numbers they had listed were cell phones, and I knew they were at work by that time in the morning, their two tiny children in day care. Did I really want to disturb them with a phone call at work? I practiced a script in my head then realized I had no idea what to say anyway. Maybe I'd wait on contacting them until they got home. I could walk over this evening, since they were in the next house downhill from me. Be a good chance to get to know them better anyway.

Catherine Sullivan and her pack of three children were next on my list. I'm acquainted with her son Randy. He must be seventeen by now. And I went to the little one's fifth birthday party a while back. Catherine likely wouldn't be home. Not to mention, she's perpetually overwhelmed between working in town and raising three challenging kids on her own. Maybe I'd wait on them, too, at least until Randy was home from school, assuming he still went to school.

Freda von Leising was next. There wasn't much point in calling her since she'd been among the bunch gathered in Helen's driveway and had already heard about the trunk incident. Besides, she was off in town buying groceries.

Marla Weisel's name appeared next. Nope, I'm not calling her. I didn't have any actual enemies in Arroyo Loco, but if I did, she'd be tops on that list. And I strongly suspect the feeling is mutual. Besides, even if I did call, she wouldn't answer once she saw my name in the display. She never does. I don't wish her any ill, but if there's a bad guy roaming our canyon and he's going to clonk anyone here with a recently liberated nine iron, Marla might be my preferred candidate. In any case, Marla was well-guarded by a less-than friendly dog, Zero.

Next name was Amanita's. Whoever put this list together was weak on the alphabet. Warten should have come before

Weisel. Either way, I wasn't voluntarily having a conversation with Amanita. True, her house is fairly isolated near the top of the hill and so might be more likely to have been chosen as a hideout by an itinerant bad guy, but there were at least two or three vacant houses in our community at that moment. The guy could be anywhere, if he was here at all. Anyway, I saw Amanita leave early this morning, so she was probably not at home to receive my phone call.

This whole phone tree thing wasn't working out. It always sounds like such a good idea, then you get started making calls and it all falls apart. Maybe Bryce had been right about holding a meeting. One quick email to the whole neighborhood and you're done.

I flipped the page over. Oh sure, Helen gets to call my best friend Nina, and Lauren, too. Lauren is always easy-going and pleasant. Why did I get stuck with the cranky end of the list? I sent a quick text to Helen.

Not calling marla you know why

There. Helen could make that call if she thinks it's that important. She doesn't necessarily get along any better with Marla, but at least Helen has a thicker skin than I. She's significantly less likely to end any conversation with Marla in a puddle of tears, the way I'm prone to do.

I tapped my phone list, deciding I was done with that task. Wondering if I should call the sheriff. The situation did not warrant a nine-one-one call, but maybe I could call the non-emergency number. It was true that Detective Muñoz and I were fairly good friends, and he even consulted with me on occasional cases, depending on the current crime he was investigating. I'm sure he wouldn't mind a quick buzz on his cell phone. Anyway, it was Thursday, Muñoz's day off. I could make the call more friendly than businesslike. Maybe ask him about the border collie puppy he and his roommate were raising.

Having convinced myself what a great idea this was, I punched the speed dial on my cell phone. Muñoz answered halfway through the first ring. He sounded breathless. I could hear some kind of a loudspeaker in the background. I made sure he knew it was me, then asked, "How are you? Where are you?"

"Men's Colony. What's up?"

"I thought Thursday was your day off."

"It is, unless a prisoner has escaped. All leave is cancelled until we find the guy."

"Is this the same guy from last night? On the news they said he was still somewhere on the prison grounds."

"If he is, we can't find him."

"What do you mean, 'if he is'? Are you thinking now he's gotten off the property?"

"Seems like the only alternative."

"So, for example, he got into the trunk of someone's car and rode off the prison grounds and could be anywhere?" As I said this, I moved around the room, checking locks on the windows.

"That's unlikely, but he doesn't appear to be here any longer."

"Okay, well, so I'm glad I called then, because ... " and I explained about the situation with Grant's trunk.

Like Grant, Muñoz insisted it would have been nearly impossible for anyone to have left the prison grounds inside an employee's trunk, but I could hear him clicking a pen and mumbling the way he does when he's writing something. He also said the puppy was fine, although driving them both nuts with needing entertainment. I welcomed him to the world of living with a border collie, and we disconnected.

Muñoz's comment about having to keep his baby border collie entertained reminded me that Scout, Shiner, and I needed a practice session on the scent work we were studying. Each dog was learning to recognize a particular scent contained in a tiny plastic vial, then to find the one small cardboard box out of eight that contained the same scent. Both dogs already excelled and were titled at sheepherding, but scent work provides great brain exercise even for older dogs, and builds self-confidence as well. We have no intention of ever working at an odor detection job, or even entering trials. We just enjoy the game. Giving both dogs a chance to succeed at finding the scent several times ate up the rest of the morning.

It was nearly time for lunch and so far I had not completed even one item on the extensive to do list I'd left on the table that morning. It would be a busy afternoon. In order to have the energy to really snap into action after lunch, I fixed myself a hearty meal of homemade tomato soup, leftover empanadas, a pile of corn chips and the last half slice of apple pie from last night.

Belatedly, I realized that much food at one sitting made me want to nap. I stumbled to the swing on the screened porch, and sat to contemplate the new garden plot to the side of the driveway.

When the county had installed our new street and sidewalks, they'd made driveway cuts at each of our homes.

Each home was allowed a cut to accommodate two cars. My gravel pad was wide enough for three, but after the county got finished, any third car would have to bump over the sidewalk curb to get parked. Diego and I decided to install xeriscape plantings and enjoy that area as a garden. Diego had already rotor-tilled the ground and helped me place the bird bath. It was my turn to purchase and install plants and a drip line. The birdbath I'd been given for my birthday sat alone in the middle of the dirt. After the boar had knocked it over last week, Diego had driven a long piece of rebar into the ground and slid the bath's hollow center over that. We'd already pencilled out a map of what plants went where, and calculated the amount of drip line and number of emitters needed. I yawned.

I tried to convince myself that buying the plants would be fun. Buying supplies for a new project is always fun. The problem with buying plants is that then you have to actually put them in the ground and water them. Other kinds of projects, you can have the fun of buying the supplies, then leave them on the dining room table until you have friends over for dinner and need to move that stuff to the garage. There the supplies sit for a year or two until you're in the mood to do the project, or the Salvation Army comes by asking for donations of household items and you can finally get that stuff out of the garage.

Plants, on the other hand, have to be planted, and right away. Dilly-dally at all, and you've got a bunch of dead plants. I yawned again. Maybe if I bought the plants, Alex and Diego would take pity and help me plant them.

I talked myself into getting in the car by promising to buy a fancy coffee in town, strictly to give me energy for the project ahead. I backed out, then pulled back into the driveway, moved the dogs from their securely fenced backyard into the house, and locked everything up tight. Nobody likes to live in a constant state of fear, but there's also no sense in taking unnecessary risks.

Shopping for plants is a lot more fun for me than shopping for clothes. By the time I'd chosen three one-gallon butterfly bushes in a variety of colors, a selection of native coastal ceanothus plants, various drought-tolerant and bird-friendly ground covers, and six coral bells for the shady area, it was almost dinner time. I lingered over an allegedly squirrel-proof bird feeder, but decided that, what with the boar already frequenting my yard, I did not need to attract any additional potentially marauding critters.

As I rounded the last curve before the entrance to Arroyo Loco Road, I was accosted by a curious sight. A crowd of about a dozen people milled on the porch and highway side of the roadhouse, and two white SUVs emblazoned with the county sheriff's decals blocked the entrance to the road. I rolled to a stop in front of Graciela's real estate office. A couple of the folks gathered by the roadhouse turned and waved. Looked to be mostly my neighbors out there.

"Yoo-who, Estela!" Freda called as I meandered toward the group. "So exciting! Look! The deputy sheriffs are here! We are all being searched!"

"Yes, Estela," Bryce added. "Thanks to you, we have to shelter in place." He circled through the group, calling, "Shelter in place, please everyone. Lockdown! Lockdown!"

Raymond had had enough. "Pipe down, Bryce. We're all already here."

"I give," I said to Freda. "What's going on?"

"Ooh, your friend the detective is here, Estela." She gave me a big sloppy wink with one eye heavily laden with mascara, and sang out the next sentence. "You know, your Detective Muñoz."

Sheesh, when would Freda ever get a clue. "He's not my Muñoz, Freda. In fact, he's someone else's Muñoz."

"Oh, phooey, he is not. Have you ever seen him with a woman? You need to get over being shy. He is so handsome!" She very nearly swooned at that, masking the sound of my teeth grinding. "Ooh, look! Here he comes now," and she gave me a rude shove in the direction of the approaching detective.

CHAPTER FIVE

"Speak of the devil, and up he pops," I said, pretending I hadn't already seen Detective Muñoz coming. He stopped and gestured for me to duck under the yellow tape stretched across the road.

I furrowed my brow. "What the heck?" I said when we had moved out of earshot.

He cleared his throat. "We never could find that escapee, and after you called about Grant's car being broken into, the sheriff thought, in the interest of prudence, we should see if he possibly did ride out here. We're searching each house, and anyplace else someone might be hiding."

"You didn't search my house, did you?"

"No, ma'am. You've got yourself some vicious-sounding watch dogs in there."

"That's good to know." I've never been sure if my border collies would bark at an intruder, or just bring him toys in hopes he would throw something for them to chase.

"Want to corral those dogs and let the deputies inside?"

"Oh. Okay, I guess I should. Although, how likely is it a bad guy is inside with the dogs?" Muñoz shrugged. He'd met my dogs on a number of occasions and apparently thought it not unlikely they would be willing to admit any bad guy who might throw a ball. Since we were going anyway, Muñoz got a deputy to move one of the SUVs, pull back the tape, and we took my plant-filled car slowly uphill. The whole village was crawling with various uniformed individuals poking under bushes in front yards and emerging from opened front doors.

"So, which is Grant's car?" Muñoz asked, looking at those we were passing.

"Oh, his car isn't here. He took it to work."

"He took the car to work? The car you think someone might have been in the trunk?" The pitch in Muñoz's voice began to climb just enough to make me feel inexplicably defensive.

"Maybe Helen could ask him to bring it back?" I said, trying to sound conciliatory.

Muñoz indicated I should never mind with a disgusted shake of his head and keyed on his radio. He ordered whoever it was who answered to locate Grant and his car, have the trunk and its contents fingerprinted, and ask Grant if anything was missing.

"Helen's golf clubs were in there," I offered, "and she says her nine iron is missing. Her nine iron and her golf gloves." We'd reached my driveway.

Muñoz extracted a notebook and stubby pencil from his pocket and wrote, his lips forming the words "nine iron."

"And her gloves," I added, to be helpful. He didn't look at me, but he did keep writing.

I took the dogs out to their yard and played with them while two fresh-faced young deputies searched the premises. I wasn't sure why the detective thought a bad guy might have gotten into my house with the dogs, considering the deputies had been afraid to try, and sure enough, they found no one inside. Muñoz then instructed them to round up everyone in town and have us gather in the roadhouse.

We didn't bother unfolding the chairs, but crowded in close as Muñoz called us to attention. I tried to stay on the outskirts, because, breaking the rules yet again, and since I had no intention of walking home alone, I had brought the dogs with me.

As the ranking member of the sheriff's department present, Detective Muñoz explained that Arroyo Loco had been thoroughly searched, and there was little reason to think the escapee was in the area anyway. "Nevertheless," he said, "as long as the escapee remains unaccounted for, it's only prudent for all residents of the county to exercise caution." He told us we should always keep our cars locked, especially because so few of us had garages in which to park those cars. The guy might especially be looking for a means to travel, and an unlocked car with a full gas tank would be a likely target.

Bryce wanted to know why the escapee wouldn't simply break into our houses and steal our car keys right out of our hands if he wanted a car that badly. Muñoz scowled and told us again to exercise caution.

"How about the dogs?" Bryce asked. "Shouldn't we have dogs searching Arroyo Loco? Estela could have her dogs search, right?" Bryce turned and gave me an encouraging nod.

Surprisingly, Muñoz did not immediately dismiss this suggestion. In fact, he acknowledged that search dogs might be a good idea, and said he could request the dogs at the prison pay us a visit. He made another notation in his book.

By the end of that little pep talk, all of us were staring at one another with uncertain eyes.

"I'm getting out of here," Amanita said, her voice a loud whisper. "This is insane. I'm packing my stuff and leaving." She made as though to go out the door, then stopped and looked at the rest of us. No one else was moving in that direction.

"So, what should we do?" I said to Muñoz. "Should we all go home, lock our cars, and stay inside until you find this guy? He might be long gone by now. You might never find him."

Detective Muñoz stared at me for one long, deep breath. I knew he didn't have any answers, and I also knew he knew I had made a good point. None of us can live our lives locked inside indefinitely. He shook his head and went outside to join the deputies standing beside their vehicles.

The rest of us trooped out and looked around. Nina headed to her house to await the locksmith expected at any moment, and a few of us lingered. Raymond and Sunshine climbed their steps and waved goodbye. Jessica mother-henned her brood across the road and into their two-story. Strength in numbers, I thought as I watched them all go. Freda, Helen, and I wandered onto Nina's porch with her.

Helen sprawled in a wicker chair, stretching her long legs out. "When's your locksmith due?"

Nina peered through her kitchen window. "*Dios mio*, he's an hour late already. What am I going to do if he doesn't get here today? I'm not staying in a house where anyone could have the key."

I offered to let Nina sleep on my couch. The couch was kind of lumpy, and maybe not as clean as it could be. We could always spread a freshly laundered sheet over it. She politely declined my offer.

Helen's eyelids were drooping to half-staff. "What about your new boyfriend? Couldn't you go stay with him?"

Nina gave a disgusted huff. "Him? I dumped him last week. What an *imbécil*."

Freda and I shot questioning glances at one another, but neither of us wanted to trigger Nina's ire by exploring the matter further.

Helen wasn't so shy. "Another loser, huh?"

"They're all losers," Nina said.

Having recently met and married Grant, Helen didn't buy that line. "Any chance you're picking the wrong ones? Men are like a box of chocolates, Nina. Any chance you're always choosing those disgusting ones with the pink filling?"

Nina narrowed her eyes. "That's exactly why I am not choosing any after this. I will sample one bite out of each one, then throw them away."

"What happens if you find a good one?" I asked. "Sure, lots of them turn out to be those yucky pink ones, but every once in a while you get nougat and walnuts. What'll you do then?"

Shaking her head, Nina said, "I'll let you know. So far, they've all turned out to be filled with pink creme. A whole box of disgusting pink ones, with deceptive candy coatings."

A white van rolled up at that moment, with a brass-colored key painted on the side. The rest of us scurried out of the way while the van's driver began unloading odd bits of equipment.

We continued on across the bridge, then slowed to a halt in front of Helen's place. Even my dogs were peering about suspiciously. They made eye contact with me, lowered their heads to gaze under nearby bushes, then crowded against my legs.

"So, what happens now?" I said. "We all go home, lock our doors, and hide out?" Freda raised her eyebrows, but neither she nor Helen had any new answers. "What a pain! What if I want to walk the dogs, or need something from my car? I'm forever needing to run out to the car for my emergency wind-up flashlight or some dad-blasted thing."

Helen shook her head slowly. "Possibly you could consider getting a second wind-up flashlight to keep in the house."

"Oh, good suggestion, Helen. Like I hadn't thought of that myself. And what do you have to suggest about letting the dogs out after dark? Do I send them out to the yard alone to take their chances, or should I go with them?"

Bryce arrived beside us in time to hear my question. "Here's what you do," he said in his most authoritative tone. "Leave the lights on very dimly inside the house. Leave the porch lights off. Turn the floodlights on over the yard. Walk the dogs to their dog door on the porch and send them through."

"Oh, don't be foolish, Bryce," Freda said. "Everyone knows you should turn every single light on to scare away a burglar." The exchanges among Helen, Bryce and Freda then devolved into a snarl of opinions, accusations, and recriminations. Our shared fear was making us all anxious and cranky.

I moved away. Yelling at each other was not going to help, and I wanted to get home and unload those plants from my car before it the sun began to set. If there's anything more deadly to a bunch of recently purchased plants than not planting them quickly enough, it's leaving them in the car too long.

The dogs and I had reached that curve between our house and the Raskins' place, where a small canyon drops off to the left, when running footsteps approached us from behind. Shiner gave out with several of his deep, threatening barks, pulling toward the coming footsteps. He was determined to get between me and the approaching danger. Although the afternoon shadows were long in the canyon, it wasn't dark yet. The hair on the back of my neck prickled as the footsteps grew closer, and I hurried a bit faster.

The thing with your dog barking a warning is, then what? The dog barks frantically. There is definitely a danger there. Like I said, then what? A warning is great, but what do you do once you've been alerted to the threat?

My heart felt like a frozen meatloaf. It was heavy, and definitely not beating. If I'd turned to look I would have seen that it was Bryce running toward his own house, but the situation and all the scary talk had me petrified. When Bryce appeared harmlessly in my peripheral vision, I tugged Shiner toward me and trotted after my fleet-footed neighbor. At least as long as I could see him ahead I didn't feel so alone.

The dogs and I reached our porch steps, discovered the screened door was unlatched again, and paused while I worked the key in the kitchen door. Irrational fear made the hair rise on the back of my neck. For no reason at all, I anticipated an attack at any second. Like cats in a fight, the fur spiked on the back of the dog's necks. At last we burst inside and I threw the deadbolt behind us. "Whew!"

On the other hand, was there possibly someone already inside with us? The deputies had searched earlier, but nothing beats a dog for scenting out an unfamiliar intruder. I gave the dogs the "search" command, then instantly remembered we had, in fact, had two unfamiliar intruders in the house earlier, in the form of the deputies themselves. Shiner made eye contact with me and ambled off in the direction of the bedroom. I thought I knew what he was going after, and it wasn't a recent escapee from prison. Sure enough, half a minute later he was back with his new stuffed pineapple. He dropped it at my feet and waited patiently for me to throw it. Scout was across the room, checking to see if anyone had thought to dump kibble in his dish. So much for my brave protectors.

A few minutes later, the kitchen door banged open behind me, and Diego and Alex stumbled in, laden with grocery bags. Everyone was safely home for the night. I decided that one of us lying awake all night was enough, and chose not to share the latest excitement going on in Arroyo Loco with my roommates. Whatever had happened in and around the trunk on Grant's Buick, no one knew for sure if any of that was related to the recent escape of a dangerous inmate from the nearby prison.

Friday morning started earlier than usual for me. I'd slept only sporadically anyway, and by six, decided there was not much point in continuing to try. I made up my mind to use the extra time to make a nice breakfast for everyone, so went out to the porch to gather the ingredients for the Denver omelettes I had my heart set on for breakfast. We'd had to utilize space in the small refrigerator out there, since, with three of us now living in the small house, the kitchen refrigerator was always full.

Anyway, that's when I discovered an entire six-pack of sodas missing. I had not noticed last night, but someone had clearly helped themselves to six cans of my generic brand ginger ale. Was this another act of mischief? Or had my teen-aged neighbor Randy prevailed on my occasionally offered generosity again? Or maybe this was simply a case of Diego and Alex getting thirsty in the middle of the night, although admittedly, that was a lot of soda for two people. I stepped back and double-checked the screened porch latch. It was unlocked again.

Diego stumbled into the kitchen just as I returned inside. He was fresh from his shower. I really wanted to ask him if he knew anything about the missing soda, though that would mean admitting I had likely left the screened door unlocked again. On the other hand, hadn't Diego and Alex been the last ones to come through that door the previous night?

Having not yet said anything about the escapee, I decided to hold fast to my policy and zipped my lip. No sense in starting this last day of the work week on a sour note.

For once, breakfast was ready in time for everyone to sit at the table to shovel it in, and still make it out to their car on time. That morning they each rolled a small suitcase down the porch steps. Their plan was to spend the weekend in the Napa wine country, leaving me to myself for a couple of days. Another good reason for me not to mention the escapee. I wanted them to have a nice weekend break and not worry about me.

I blew each a kiss and waved goodbye. No one was more surprised than I when the door burst open a few seconds later and Diego stormed inside.

"*¡Dios maldito!* Some damn fool broke into my car!"

Alex tiptoed inside behind him. "They broke out one of the back windows. Totally smashed it."

Diego searched for something on his phone, then turned and marched back out. He focused and began to photograph the rear driver's side window.

"Was anything stolen?" I said to Alex, thinking again about those sodas. We both gazed at the damaged window.

Alex followed Diego down the steps. "*Querido,* was anything stolen from inside?"

"What? Oh. You know this window alone is going to cost my whole deductible to fix, don't you?"

"Good day to be in the auto-glass replacement business," I muttered to myself. Between Grant's rear window yesterday, and Diego's today, someone was going to be busy.

Chunks of glass tinkled to the ground when Diego opened the rear door of his almost new Prius. He peered inside.

"Anything gone?" I said again.

Diego started to say no, then, in a puzzled tone he said, "*Dios maldito,* my gym bag is gone. Why would someone break into my car to steal a gym bag? All it had in it was a flimsy towel, flip-flops, and an old yoga mat."

"You're sure that's all you were carrying?" I said. "Maybe someone thought you had something more valuable in there?"

Diego shook his head. "No. A razor, deodorant, the usual junk. My old sweat pants. Nothing worth breaking a window to get."

"Of course, no one could tell what was in there without breaking in," Alex added.

This was one of those too-big-to-be-a-coincidence things. Two cars broken into, two nights in a row. Each time, sporting equipment is stolen, or at least gear associated with sports. Might this really be the work of frustrated neighborhood kids?

"Can you tell if they tried to steal the car?" I said. "You know, like wires ripped loose or something?"

In a defeated tone, Diego said, "No. You can't hot-wire a Prius. They've got this computerized ignition system. The only way to steal a Prius is to either steal the key, or tow the whole thing away on a flat bed. If someone wanted to steal a car here, they would have taken yours."

Since he'd mentioned it, I sidled alongside my slightly dinged Subaru and tried the door. Locked. No windows broken. The only thing visible inside to steal was a wadded up grease-stained take-out bag from Pacito's Taqueria. Guess there's more than one way to ensure your car is not a target for theft.

I offered them my car to get to their jobs, but Diego sighed and said he'd drive his damaged one and try to get the window fixed while he was at work. Possibly he could get one of those mobile auto-glass companies to repair it. His plan apparently did not include reporting the break-in to the county sheriff. I just had to hope they would make the hour journey to their work location safely in spite of the busted out window.

CHAPTER SIX

Diego and Alex finally drove off to work, and I helped myself to a fresh cup of coffee, settling on the porch swing to enjoy it and contemplate the planting job ahead. After a minute or two, a tiny goldfinch flitted onto the edge of the birdbath. I knew it was a goldfinch because that's one of the few birds I had learned to identify on sight in the months since I had adopted my new birding hobby. Two minutes later, she was joined by a second, and then a third goldfinch. One of them stepped gingerly into the shallow water and began fluttering her wings. Water splashed everywhere in a fountain of tiny droplets. The other two birds got so drenched they had no need to take their own baths.

I was so focused on that scene, captivated by nature, I didn't even notice movement beyond the bird bath. Then my focus shifted and I saw, out on the new sidewalk and also entranced by the display the birds were putting on, the most curious human creature I had ever seen. No more than fifteen inches high, he was all head with round ears that looked like knees on each side, and small red feet poking out from underneath. Our eyes came together and his expression shifted to one of alarm. His strange form unfolded to reveal a tiny boy dressed in summer pajamas and wearing miniature red crocs. Looked like the Raskins' older boy. He couldn't possibly be more than two years old. And he was as fascinated by the bathing birds as was I.

The distinctive two-syllable hail of a mother calling her child in from play sounded, "Eeee-lie!" The tiny moppet turned and toddled out of sight. That reminded me that I had not called the Raskin's yesterday, as had been my assignment. Between the incident at Grant's house and now the theft from Diego's car, I really should let them know what was going on before they left for work again.

I don't normally go calling on neighbors so early, but I quickly leashed the dogs and headed that way. Thought I should probably tell the rest of the neighbors about Diego's theft, too, although I dreaded the excitement that would create. The whole brouhaha might leave precious little time for planting my new garden.

Jeannie Raskin was pulling pants on her young son when I arrived on their doorstep. She was all set to go off to work except for changing out of her bunny-rabbit slippers and finishing those last few bites of toast. A tiny baby waved fists and feet at me from his reclining seat propped on the table when Jeannie invited me into the kitchen. The counters were cluttered with brightly colored warming dishes containing dabs of dried-on goo, and grape juice stained plastic sippy cups.

She waved me toward a chair and offered coffee, but I didn't want to slow her preparations, and in any case, the seat of that chair was already decorated with shiny fingerprints that looked suspiciously sticky. Even my dogs, nestled up to my legs, seemed reluctant to sit down. While she tackled the mess, I explained about the thefts in the neighborhood. Jeannie seemed surprised to hear we had been having problems, although her mouth adopted a thin-lipped angry frown.

"That's terrible," she said. "Such a shame." We both shook our heads to indicate our disgust with the sad state of affairs. "That does remind me," she went on, "I have been meaning to thank you for bringing in Eli's toys every evening. That's been very kind of you. We're swamped with two babies."

I ran her words through my mind, but could make no sense of them. "What do you mean?" I finally said.

"You know, bringing Eli's tricycle up to the porch, and gathering those toys he leaves all over the place. I don't have time to track everything down after work. You are the one bringing those onto the porch, right? You're the only one we ever see walking past here."

"As much as I'd like to take credit for the good deed, I have no idea what you're talking about. It wasn't me."

"Huh."

"Must have been someone else."

"Yeah, but who? Every morning we go out and all the toys are collected together on the porch. Who else could it be?"

We both thought about that for a minute.

"Maybe DeVon or Chamise, Delia's kids?" I suggested. "They're both good kids, and Delia keeps a tight rein on both of them, their manners and what not. They're right next door to you."

"Yes, Delia came over and introduced herself and her kids when we first moved in, but I've not talked to any of them since," Jeannie said. "Doesn't seem like it would be them." She paused, thinking. "If it's not you, then it's kind of creepy. Some stranger coming into our yard at night putting my kids' toys away? That's creepy, right?"

"Kind of," I agreed. "Especially considering everything else going on in Arroyo Loco. I gather this toy pick-up routine has been going on for quite some time?"

"Oh, yes. Ever since we first moved here, really. Several months at least." Something else troubled her, but she hesitated.

"What?"

"I'm wondering, is all," she said. "The toys are collected, which is great, but then, last night my husband's crocs went missing. They were covered in mud so I made him leave them on the front porch. I told him I'd clean them today, and well, this morning I noticed they were gone. I thought maybe he took them, for some reason, or moved them. Let me text him."

While she buried her head in her phone, balancing Eli on her hip so she pull on his shoes, I thought about what she'd said. The nightly neat-nik who had been picking up the Rankin's toys for months, and now the disappearing crocs, was probably not any prison escapee recently emerged from Grant's trunk. Those activities had to have been perpetrated by someone else.

Jeannie already had one arm loaded with a fully packed diaper bag and her travel mug, and cradled Eli in the other when her phone dinged. She scooped that with a free finger and she read as she trotted toward her car. I wondered for a moment if she had forgotten the baby still sucking a fist in his car seat on the kitchen table, but she was back in a flash. "Nope," she said. "He didn't move his shoes. Someone must have taken them. Or possibly Eli wandered off with them." On this trip, she carried the baby, a briefcase, and a second diaper bag, her car keys dangling from the side of her mouth. I held the bag while she buckled the baby securely into the car.

"I'll tell you what," I said, "I'll keep an eye out when I'm walking the dogs past here. Maybe one evening I'll see someone." I excused myself to go talk to the other neighbors and Jeannie's car backed out fast, late to get her kids to day care and herself to her part-time job.

For once, I had a lucky day. No one answered the door at Delia's house, and both Freda and Helen were not at home either. I didn't want to interrupt Lauren in her upstairs office at her house. She was probably immersed in an important project. Reasoning that I could tell everyone about the theft from Diego's car at our next gathering, the dogs and I trotted home where I got busy digging a hole for one of the butterfly bushes. It wasn't until later that I learned why none of my immediate neighbors were at home that morning.

I could have dug all the holes at once, but reasoned that, given my natural-born grace and nimbleness, I'd probably break an ankle stepping in one hole while digging another. One hole at a time would eventually get them all dug and the plants installed. Besides, if I approached this task in an inefficient manner, someone else might come along and help me out. Sadly, that someone would not be Diego or Alex, as they were off for their romantic weekend in Napa beginning after work this evening.

I did consider trying to persuade one of the dogs to dig a deep, neat round hole, but there is a limit to the cleverness of dogs, even border collies. Or maybe they're too smart to get snookered.

Somewhere amid this pleasant diversion, that *whine-whine-whine* of a loose fan belt assailed me again. Amanita's green sedan drew close beside me. Her car was stuffed to the gills with books, boxes, and full black garbage bags. She rolled her passenger window down and glared at me. As the window lowered, a colorful box proclaiming that it contained an Osterizer teetered on top of the pile, threatening to slide out. I secured the box deeper inside the window before it could fall and smash my foot.

"Those better be approved drought-tolerant plants you're putting in," she said, pointing.

"Oh, of course!" I smiled.

"I know you didn't get approval from the planting committee, Estela. In fact, I know you didn't even submit a planting plan to the committee. Is that a ceanothus I see? Those rarely do well in our coastal fog. I don't want to drive by and see a lot of unsightly dead plants in two weeks. You should have gotten approval first, Estela."

"Oh, that's a Julia Phelps ceanothus. They're native to this region." I smiled broadly and tightened my grip on the shovel, willing myself not to swing it. "The birds love the cover it provides." Breaking eye contact, I went back to digging. Amanita and I maintain a fragile truce most of the time, based primarily on my ability to ignore her.

To my horror, the next sound I heard was Amanita's parking brake ratcheting on. Her door squealed open. She came around the small sedan, hands firmly on hips, and surveyed my project.

"This is a complete violation of the HOA rules, Estela. I should cite you right now."

I stopped and drew myself to my full height, shovel at the ready. I may be short, but if I really suck in my gut I can make myself at least a half a head taller than that stumpy little Amanita. I glared back. Considered pointing out all of the HOA rules with which I was currently in full compliance. Wisely decided maybe this wasn't the time for an attempt at comic relief.

"This garden area has been carefully planned and every plant in it will be drought-tolerant." I hoped my tone indicated that, while my argument was well-reasoned, I was fully prepared to follow it up with a nicely placed whack to the forehead with the shovel. I would never do such a thing, of course, but didn't think there would be any harm in hinting that I might.

Amanita's voice took on the slightest edge of a whine. "You still should have gotten approval. We have to protect our property values here in Arroyo Loco. That's what the rules are for, is to protect property values. And that's what our planting committee does. It's for your own good you know, to protect your property values."

She stopped talking and I continued to glare. Often, no words are better than the wrong ones, especially in light of the fact that, in Amanita's view, her words are the only right ones.

"Besides, even if they are drought-tolerant, plants there will use more water than before."

My glared shifted to incredulous. Yes, it's certainly true that even my new drought-tolerant plants will use more water than the previous graveled parking pad. A number of steaming retorts flared through my mind, mostly suggestions about turning all of Arroyo Loco into a graveled parking pad, and then disbanding her precious planting committee altogether. On the other hand, it is true that native plantings often do use even more water during their first year or two, until they are established. But I wasn't giving Amanita an inch. Give her an inch and she will take that proverbial mile.

"They are all native California coastal plants," I said through gritted teeth. The knuckles I had gripping the shovel handle whitened.

She cut a quick glance to my hand on the shovel and began to ease back across the front of her car.

"They might be natives, Estela, but the planting committee never approved them. They're illegal natives!" With that, she scurried behind the wheel, popped the parking brake, and rolled away, the engine still whirring.

I took several long, deep, cleansing yoga breaths, and continued with my task. One of the problems with those kinds of noxious encounters is how long it takes me to calm down afterwards. Digging in the dirt helped. I'd just finished tucking the first butterfly bush into its hole, complete with a soil amendment of worm castings, and a good dousing with seaweed extract for root growth, when I realized I was in danger of missing lunch. I hurried inside and grilled myself a nice cheese sandwich and a bowl of fresh peaches from the farmer's market. It was such a warm and beautiful late summer day, I left the kitchen door open for ventilation.

Predictably, after that satisfying lunch, I became drowsy and needed a rest. Really though, what did it matter if I took a few moments for a power nap before tackling that next butterfly bush? Diego wouldn't be home for three more days, so I'd have plenty of time to get everything planted before he returned and he'd never know the difference.

I crawled into my recliner with my book, kidding myself that maybe I would make good use of the time by reading instead of napping. Sleep overtook me before I'd even had a chance to open the book.

Generally, when I fall asleep in the recliner during the day, my singing bird clock trills me awake in no longer than an hour. So I know I had not been asleep for any longer than that when a creak out on the porch awakened me. That was the unmistakable sound of a large body trying to sneak up on me. Why were my dogs not barking?

I am not one of those people who awaken from any period of sleep, especially a day time one, perky and ready to leap into action. I gave the situation some thought, waiting for my head to clear. The door was safely locked, right? No, I remembered, the kitchen door was wide open and the porch door was unlatched.

The dogs were near me, right? No, they were in the back yard, and I was pretty sure I'd closed their dog door so they wouldn't pester me to let them come out front and help with my planting project. Still, if a stranger was creeping into my house, those dogs would normally have noticed and started barking. That was the thought that finally propelled me, roaring into action. If someone had done something to my dogs I was prepared to kill with my bare hands.

Leaping from my recliner, I yelled, "What the heck is going on here!"

Helen jumped back about three feet and nearly tripped backwards over the threshold.

"Whaaa … ," she said. "You scared me to death! I found the door wide open and heard someone breathing in that chair. You scared the wits out of me!"

"You scared me, too! Why didn't you call out or knock or something?"

"I thought it might be that escapee in the chair, what with the door standing wide open! Why are you sleeping with the door open? I did let the dogs out here, thinking they would wake whoever was in the recliner!"

"Okay, let's stop yelling at each other then, shall we?"

Shiner peered from behind Helen's legs. No wonder the dogs weren't barking. Helen was a friend. All the yelling was freaking the dogs out, but until that started they had been quietly greeting their friend Helen.

"I'll stop yelling if you will," she said. "Anyway, I did try to call on your mobile, and even texted, but no one answered. I got scared that something might have happened to you. That's why I came over. And then I found the door open … and someone in your chair. Sheesh, Estela."

I searched the surrounding surfaces for my cell phone. Maybe it was still in my bag in the bedroom. With the ringer turned off. "Sorry. Guess I didn't hear it."

Helen flipped her eyebrows at me, then explained her mission. "I wanted to tell you that we had another act of vandalism last night. Someone broke into Lauren's house. At least we think it was last night. Freda called me this morning all hysterical because more of her vegetables had been, well, let's say picked. She says stolen. I say picked. I went over to calm her down and we walked out to her garden. From there, we saw Lauren's back door standing open. Looks like the lock was, you know, kicked open."

"Good grief! Was anyone hurt?"

"No, we don't think so. Lauren, you know, she and Kelly are often away overnight. They stay in town at Kelly's place most of the time. Don't suppose you have the phone number there?"

I shook my head. Why would Helen think I might have Lauren's new girlfriend's phone number? "Doesn't Lauren have a mobile number?" I stepped to my junk drawer, pulled out my Arroyo Loco phone list, and slid my finger along until I got to Lauren's name. "Did you try this number?"

"I thought that was the number inside her house. You think it's her mobile number?"

"Worth a try," I said dialing. "Hello? Lauren? Helen wants to tell you something." I offered the handset to Helen, who explained the situation. From the half of the conversation I could hear, evidently, Freda freaked out when she saw Lauren's door open, the lock broken away from the jamb, and insisted they call nine-one-one. When they didn't get an immediate response to their call, she persuaded Helen to accompany her to the sheriff's substation in town to report the crime.

That's doubtlessly where they both had been when I went looking for them this morning. Less observant than usual, I had not noticed anything amiss at Lauren's house. The remainder of Freda and Helen's morning had been spent trying to locate Lauren, and then eventually watching a couple of deputies search her house. No bodies, alive or dead, were found inside, and very little damage. A few drawers were pulled open and left that way, and the kitchen cupboards had been rifled for anything readily edible. According to Helen, Lauren's kitchen floor was now a mess of torn packaging.

CHAPTER SEVEN

Helen was concluding her report when Bryce arrived at my porch steps. He already knew about the break-in, and was visibly annoyed to have Helen beat him to telling me the story. He also carried a clipboard with a hand-written petition on it urging yet another homeowners referendum to install a gate at the entrance to Arroyo Loco, and calling for the placement of security cameras. A few signatures were already listed on what he called his "grassroots" petition, although from my cursory glance the only signatories appeared to be members of Bryce's immediate family.

I declined the opportunity to sign. I believe my opinion on living under twenty-four hour surveillance behind a locked gate has already been adequately expressed. "If I want to live in a prison I'll make sure to commit some juicy crime to get there," I told him.

"Well, nertz," Bryce said. He left in a huff, as Helen watched, shaking her head.

"That's not the half of it, either," she said. "Graciela is now walking the neighborhood with that nasty gun of hers strapped to her waist."

"I presume she knows that's illegal in California."

"Well, I don't know about that one way or the other. I'm just telling you, she's armed to the teeth and says she'll shoot to kill. Ever since we elected her president of the homeowners association, she thinks she's the new sheriff in town. She's trying to talk Christopher into buying a gun too. I think she's still really mad about that paint on her house, and what it said."

"Yes, we are all still mad about that. It was a heck of a job to get it cleaned and painted over, too. You can still see where it happened." I heaved a big sigh and said, "Who would do such a thing?"

"And why," Helen added.

"I know. I keep asking myself why people would pile on when there's already enough ugliness in the world." We were interrupted by Freda clumping up my steps in her muumuu accessorized now with brown suede cowboy boots.

After taking a moment to catch her breath, Freda spoke. "*Guten tag,* my dears." She turned to me. "I suppose Helen told you about poor Lauren's house? Terrifying."

I nodded. Really, what could I say?

"And it is worse. I certainly hope you were not expecting me to bring you any produce from my garden, because now it is all stolen. Four bee-you-ti-ful green bell peppers, two fat zucchini, and the rest of the tomatoes, all gone."

Helen and I made the appropriate consoling noises, but there was no denying that all three of us were beginning to boil. As long as they were both sitting on my porch, I took the opportunity to tell them about Diego's car being broken into, and the theft of his gym bag. In the cold light of day, that story didn't seem so sinister as it had early that morning when it was first discovered. Kids breaking in to get a gym bag possibly containing some valued piece of sporting equipment seemed plausible, although that smashed window was more than a minor annoyance. I decided to supplement that story with the one about my likely-to-have-been stolen sodas.

"Don't tell Diego about those stolen sodas, though," I said. "The screened door to the porch was left unlocked and that was possibly my fault. He'll get annoyed with me for not locking the door, but you know, I don't like to live behind too many locked doors. How would I get out in a hurry if there was a fire or something?"

Helen and Freda nodded their agreement and concern.

"Something is going on here in our little village," Freda said. "Do you think, perhaps, it could be that prison escapee? Is he causing all of these crimes here?"

I started to answer. "No. Several of those, what you are calling crimes, those occurred before the prisoner had even escaped custody, including, you know, the first theft of your tomatoes."

Freda was not placated. She was off on a tear with her theory.

"Ooh, and that is why he is stealing my vegetables! He is hungry! And your sodas, too, Estela."

Helen was skeptical. "You're suggesting this escapee is subsisting now on a diet of cherry tomatoes and ginger ale?"

"And zucchini and peppers." Freda huffed in defense of her idea. "He must be eating something. Why not vegetables and soda?"

Helen's eyebrows popped again, and she gazed across the road for a minute. The she scowled. "Well, you are right about one thing. I think something bigger than we realized before is going on here. And you know I don't think everyone getting guns is the answer, but we need to do something!"

I had to agree with her. "But what can we do?"

"For starters, we should start a night watch. Most of this stuff seems to be happening at night, so we should take turns keeping watch all night."

"How would that work?" I said. "One night something happens at Graciela's or Nina's house. The next night it is Freda's or Lauren's. And even way at this end of the road at my place."

"Someone will have to march up and down the hill." Freda pointed back and forth. "Up and down all night long. And behind my house, too, where I am growing my garden."

Helen nodded enthusiastically. "Yes! Could you patrol with your dogs, Estela? The dogs could cover a lot more ground, and take down the culprit when you spotted him. Or her."

At least three different emoticons could have adequately expressed my emotions at that moment, but words escaped me.

"No, huh?" Helen said.

I shook my head. "I do think we ought to reconsider having a meeting, though. Maybe someone else will have a better idea."

"Yes." Freda nodded sadly. "We are having a crime spree for sure. Even that Muñoz cannot help us. He said to keep our eyes open for anything unusual. Now everything is unusual."

A squealing sound from out on the road startled us out of our conversation. We turned as Bryce reappeared, strolling downhill and steering his father Ernie in a battered wheelchair. In his lap, Ernie clutched a brown cardboard box. Various cords and electrical devices peeped over the edge of the box. Helen waved them over. Bryce tipped the wheelchair like you would a baby's stroller, and executed a sharp right turn. This caused Ernie to yelp in surprise and clutch at the cardboard box tipping precariously in his lap. When they arrived in front of the porch, Helen explained our thoughts about calling a neighborhood meeting. Sooner rather than later seemed like a good time, so we decided on six that evening when almost everyone should be home from work. Great, I thought, this is exactly how I hoped to spend my next-to-last Friday night before the semester started at the university and I had to go back to work. Bryce agreed to send out the email calling the meeting after he'd delivered Ernie to his destination.

"What'cha got there in the box?" Helen asked Ernie.

"Uh, stuff." Ernie looked into the box. Seemed like he didn't really want to answer Helen's question.

"What stuff, Ernie?" Helen wasn't giving up that easily. "Looks like some electronic gizmos in there. What's it for?"

"Uh, I threw some extra stuff in here. Raymond wants to install a camera on his porch, so I threw some extra stuff I had laying around in here."

"Yeah," Bryce said. "You know. Raymond wants a camera pointing at Nina's porch so he can see if anyone tries to break into her house, what with the key stolen and all. Nina thinks it might be that Martin, her daughter's former boyfriend who stole the key. She's afraid he might try to get inside."

Freda scrunched her brow in confusion. "I thought that boy went to prison. Did he get out of prison already? *Mein gott*, is he the man who escaped from the prison! Could that be? Should we tell everyone it could be him?"

And this is exactly how rumors get started in Arroyo Loco. Without another word, I slunk into my kitchen and closed the door, leaving my guests to let themselves out.

Since I was inside anyway, I took the opportunity to finish off the tail-end of a Sara Lee chocolate loaf cake that was only going to go bad sooner or later in the freezer. After an hour or so, I figured the coast was clear, and went back out and started digging the second hole. It was barely two shovelfuls deep when the canyon erupted with screaming bellows from somewhere downhill. Sounded a lot like Helen. Who needs a phone or emails with lungs like those? Dropping the shovel, I took off to find the source of the screams. You may want to note that I left in a hurry, and thus did not take the time to latch my screened door, secure my dogs in the house, or even lock the new kitchen deadbolt.

By the time I got there, neighbors were streaming to the side of Helen's house, heading toward the back yard. I was among the late arrivals, which included Bryce, who is usually first on the scene. He wielded a two-foot long hunk of lumber. Graciela's silver BMW arrived last. She emerged from behind the wheel with a thick belt looped over her shoulder from which hung a leather holster with the grip of a large handgun peeping out. She looked like a modern-day, fashionably attired version of Pancho Villa—minus the mustache and the horse. I briefly wondered if I should have brought a make-shift weapon of my own.

The scene behind Helen's house was chaotic and it was difficult at first to determine exactly what had caused the ruckus. Helen paced wildly about, tearing at her hair and wailing. Something about her cats. I said a quick prayer that no one had injured those cats. A few acts of mischief were one thing. Even a couple of broken car windows. But hurting anyone was a whole other kettle of fish. That I would not tolerate.

I reached out to Freda as she trotted past me to see if she could explain the problem, but she continued to run. She was attempting to comfort Helen whenever she was able to catch up to the much larger woman. Lauren stood to the side, looking as helpless as I felt.

I sidled up to her. "Lauren! I'm so sorry about your house. I hope nothing valuable was taken." Even as I said it, I knew that was a lame thing to say. What could be more valuable than a person's sense of safety in their own home? And that had obviously been taken from Lauren. She did look slightly shell-shocked.

I decided to change the subject. "What's going on here? Do you know? What happened?"

"See there?" Lauren pointed at the rear-most side of the wire "catio" Helen had constructed on her back concrete deck. The approximately six foot square cage provided Helen's cats with a place to get outside and enjoy fresh air and the sights and sounds of nature without violating our HOA guideline that domestic cats remain inside the domicile at all times. This was not a rule, you understand, only a guideline.

A large gash had been cut through the wire of the catio, and the mesh pulled back, creating an opening wide enough that even Helen's fattest cat could have easily made an escape. And apparently he had, because Helen's wails resolved into a keening variation of his name, "Mocha."

I am sure that Helen was genuinely upset. She loves her cats and tries her best to take care of them. However, this was not the first time Mocha had gone missing. In fact, if I recalled correctly, when that cat had escaped previously, he had lived on his own on the hillside behind Arroyo Loco for a matter of several months. I would be the last person who would want that dad-blasted feline to be roaming the hills killing songbirds, but given his history, the chances of being able to keep Mocha corralled inside seemed less than good. Especially not when his escapes were abetted by a human cutting holes through the wire of his catio.

"Oh, Mocha!" Helen wailed, then she caught my gaze. I did remember something about one of my dogs helping tree Mocha during his last escapade. I also recalled that his assistance was unappreciated by Helen. Now she seemed to be pleading for my help. "He's gone for good, Estela. Unless you can help me find him, he's gone for good this time."

I looked at the hillsides surrounding the back of our houses. Covered with oak trees, rocks and bushes, there were a million places a clever cat could hide. And no self-respecting cat was going to return to enjoy Helen's hospitality as long as she continued to cry out in that ear-splitting tone.

"We'll try, Helen." I nodded and smiled in my most reassuring way. "Are the rest of the cats okay?"

"Yes, yes, they're fine. They're all inside eating. That's when I noticed Mocha was gone. When I fed them. Then I came out and saw this, this ... " and we lost Helen again to another protracted wail.

Our Pancho Villa wannabe neighbor, Graciela, stepped forward. "What I want to know is who did this!" She placed her palm over the butt of that ugly looking gun threateningly. "I've had enough of this so-called mischief. We have every right to defend ourselves and I intend to do exactly that."

This was followed by an uncomfortable silence. Nefarious acts were certainly occurring at an alarming rate in our village, but so far nothing had risen to the level where anyone, with the possible exception of Graciela, would actually want to shoot the culprit or culprits.

"There's no one here to shoot, Graciela," I said. "Go home and put that gun away. Loaded or unloaded, it's against the law in California to openly carry a handgun." I was tired of having to explain this to my neighbors, and I sounded it.

"Yes," Freda added. "Take it home before you shoot one of us."

"Or that prison escapee grabs it from you and shoots you," Helen added.

Graciela tightened her lips so hard they almost disappeared, turned abruptly, and marched toward the front yard.

When she was out of earshot, Lauren said, "Is she really disappointed she doesn't get to shoot anyone?" Lauren shook her head as she also wandered away.

Bryce was examining the cut wire closely, trying to push the opening closed and poking at the sharp points of raw wire. "When do you think this was done?" he asked Helen.

Helen sighed. "I don't know. I found it this way just now, so possibly earlier this morning. Possibly while Freda and I were at the sheriff's office."

"Not when it was light already, though, yes?" Freda joined in.

Helen leaned over and looked closely at the cut. "Yes, that's correct Freda. Grant is awake by five. He would have seen if someone had been out here while he was still home."

"But it could have been cut in the middle of the night?" I said.

"I don't see how," Helen said. "Our bedroom is right there." She pointed at the window no more than six feet over our heads. "We would have heard the snipping when the wire was cut."

That was a dilemma.

"Plus, you know what else," Bryce said, "we are all on the lookout for strangers. Whoever did this had to be someone who could move through the neighborhood without us being suspicious. Someone we all know. Especially if it was done during the daylight."

That sent a chill through everyone present. We shot each other suspicious glances.

"One of us," Freda added, completely unnecessarily.

Without a word, we eased slightly apart. Bryce turned and trotted off after Graciela.

"Hold the phone," I said, looking again at the cut. "Something's fishy here, Helen. This cage was cut once before, right?"

Wariness tinged her reply, and she dragged the word out. "Yes."

"I'm not saying we shouldn't take this seriously, Helen. I'm only pointing out the cage wasn't exactly cut this time. This time someone pulled out the wire you used to repair the previous cut."

"So what? Mocha is still gone."

"I know, sweetie, and I will help you try to find him. This might be a clue, is all I'm saying. For one thing, this previous cut might have been done any time, night or day, right?"

Helen tightened her lips and nodded. "And even if it was done at night, Grant and I might not have heard anything. No snipping."

"Right," I said. "The thing is, though, the repair wire was almost certainly removed by someone who knew it was there. If a person didn't already know it was there, they probably wouldn't have even noticed it."

"She's right!" Freda said. "Who would know about that?"

Helen gave that some thought. "I knew, of course. Bryce and I put it there. And I guess Grant knew, but neither of us would have let Mocha out like that."

"So, Bryce would know," I said. "And whoever cut the cage the first time would know." I glanced at those remaining, trying to avoid eye contact and at the same time assessing potential signs of guilt. I hear that can be done by noticing shifty eyes and so on, but not usually by me. "Okay then," I said, dropping my hands in defeat. "I'll see everyone at the meeting tonight."

"Yes," Helen said. "If Bryce remembers to send the email."

CHAPTER EIGHT

When I returned to the front of Helen's house, Graciela was still there. She and Christopher had their heads bent together talking quietly and looking over Graciela's gun. Good, just what we need, one more trigger-happy resident of Arroyo Loco.

"Have you folks heard about the meeting tonight?" I rudely interrupted.

Graciela's eyes widened. "Tonight? Should we really be out after dark? I mean, under the circumstances."

"Six o'clock," I said. "It's not dark until after eight. We should be done by then."

"Did you consider consulting the homeowners association president before you arranged this so-called meeting? And where will it be? Who knows what might happen to our homes while we're all busy inside the roadhouse?"

She had a point there. We are all so used to our canyon village being peaceful, I, for one, hadn't thought about all of our places being left insecure and empty while we met.

"We should meet outside," she suggested, "like on the porch of the roadhouse where we can keep eyes on our houses."

"That's a great idea," Christopher chimed in. "How about in the park?"

Located adjacent to the park, his home would be easy to keep an eye on from that location. Graciela's home and business were visible from the porch of the roadhouse. They both seemed more concerned about watching out for their own homes than anyone else's. I decided not to point that out. I am the first to admit that I tend to suffer from a largely unwarranted faith in the existence of an altruistic human nature, so I surprised even myself with these cynical thoughts. It is possible I have been spending too much time lately with Helen. I decided to let my faith reassert itself by not saying anything and assume the self-centeredness of their logic would eventually dawn on them.

"Hmm."

"Well, what do you suggest, Estela? Shall we meet in the middle of the road and walk along while we talk?" Graciela's snide tone wasn't earning any goodwill from me.

"Hey, that's a great idea," Bryce said. We both stared at him in disbelief. "Not to meet that way, I don't mean, but we could have a patrol going through the neighborhood while we are meeting."

Christopher nodded. "Good idea, Bryce."

Bryce puffed his chest out to twice its normal size. He noticed Helen and Freda coming into the front yard. "Hey, you guys! We're going to have a patrol! Want to be in it?"

I didn't want to burst Bryce's balloon, but as good an idea as that patrol might be, he was forgetting something. "Wait a minute, Bryce. The same people we need at the meeting can't also be in the patrol."

"Oh, right." He was crestfallen. "But I wanted to be in the patrol."

Graciela had a bright idea. "We could get the teenagers to patrol while we're meeting. They're always hanging out somewhere together anyway. Now all we have to do is get them some kind of weapons … "

"Whoa, hold your horses, Graciela," I said. "Getting the teenagers to patrol might be a good idea, but you went too far with the weapons. All they'll really need will be their phones so they can call for help."

"Yes!" Freda said. "Estela is correct. Only their cell phones. And possibly something to eat."

"A good hearty meal," Bryce suggested. "An army marches on its stomach, you know. I've heard that somewhere."

"Yes, well … " Freda was not so sure. "I could bake a nice batch of *spitzbuben*, or a few dozen *blechkuchen*. Possibly some *apfelstrudel*. I will have to see what I have in the freezer. For ingredients, you understand." She shot me a wary glance, no doubt hoping I wouldn't remember that, if the truth is told, most of her delicious baked goods came from the European bakery in town, and not from Freda's own oven.

"That's very generous of you," I said. "Maybe you could make some for the meeting, too?"

Helen shook her head. "Oh, brother. Here we go again with another pot luck. And I don't even have a car to get to the market today."

When I turned back to the group, Graciela was staring evenly at me, tapping her foot. "Weapons, Estela? If those kids catch whoever is committing all these crimes, they're not going to have time to stand there texting about it. This guy is breaking into cars and houses now. He means business, and our patrol should mean business, too."

"Uh, but guns?" Christopher said. Graciela turned her glare to him. He scratched at his blonde crew cut and tipped his head in a hemming and hawing gesture. "I don't know, Graciela. Those kids are pretty young and inexperienced to be carrying guns."

"I should say not!" Helen had gotten wind of the idea. "You give any one of us a gun, including you, Graciela … " and Helen gave Graciela a look so black you'd have thought the sun had disappeared for a moment, "and someone is going to shoot one of us neighbors! No guns! I thought we told you to take that lethal thing home!"

"You can't tell me what to do! You can keep your lily-livered liberal politics to yourself, Helen!" Graciela took an aggressive step forward, putting herself face-to-bosom with the much larger woman.

Well, shoot. Why do I always have to be the voice of reason? A knock down drag out fight could be just the ticket we needed to release the tension in Arroyo Loco. Of course I knew better. "Okay, you two. Take it easy. No one is telling you what to do, Graciela, but you have to take that firearm home and secure it. That's the law. How would it look for the homeowners association president to be hauled away for violating state law?"

Graciela stepped back. She gave me a disgusted look and turned toward her car, mumbling something disparaging about state law. At the last minute, she snagged Christopher's elbow and dragged him away with her, still whispering.

For my part, I couldn't help but wonder how the truth about the likelihood of an accidental shooting could not have already penetrated the brain of an otherwise intelligent woman. I wonder where she gets her news. We watched, saddened, in silence, as she climbed into her BMW and backed out, leaving Christopher standing alone.

"That's a good idea," Helen said. "You know, about the teenagers doing patrols." Not one to hold a grudge, Helen had already forgotten the incident. "And you know what else? We should get some guard dogs. Wouldn't guard dogs be a great idea, Estela?"

"Um, maybe." I wasn't so sure. "They're expensive, you know."

Helen nodded. "I was thinking we could possibly rent a couple. You know, for a day or two. A couple of those really big mean-looking ones."

Bryce looked worried. "Like Cujo, you mean?"

Freda shivered all over. "Oh, no, I don't think so."

"How expensive?" Helen wanted to know, not that easily deterred.

"Hundreds, at least," I said. "Maybe thousands. Those dogs are highly trained."

"Thousands!"

"And not to mention, our town isn't fenced, so you'd have to hire professional handlers, too."

Helen's eyes widened even further.

I almost had her convinced to drop the idea. And, for the *coup de grace* I delivered my final point. "And what about, they might catch Mocha while they were out there patrolling?"

"Okay, okay. Forget that plan," Helen said. "Any chance we could use our own dogs?" She turned a speculative eye at me, then glanced away. "I was thinking about Zero, for example."

She referred to Marla's untrained and reliably vicious basenji. In uncertain circumstances, even Marla was afraid of that dog.

"Yeah," Bryce said. "Zero's a guard dog, right?"

"What are you two talking about?" I said. "You want to turn Zero loose in the neighborhood? My guess is, not only would he get Mocha, he'd get the rest of our dogs, several small children, and couple of us as well. Zero doesn't know a bad guy from a friend. He's an indiscriminate biter."

"Okay, then," Helen said, "one or two of our less vicious dogs." She gave me another look.

"You can forget Shiner and Scout," I said. "They might find the bad guy, but they'd be just as likely to herd all of us into a corner, exactly like they do with the sheep. Anyway, I'm not letting them out to roam. A four hundred pound boar might step on them."

"Or Graciela would shoot them," Helen added.

"How about Itches?" Bryce said, referring to Sunshine Rainbow's itinerant beagle.

I laughed. "Itches would find him if he looks like a fox, then go baying after him, or get distracted by Mocha."

Bryce was getting into the spirit of the idea. "Tippy would buddy up with him and they'd go off and do even more mischief."

"So we're back to Zero," Helen said, "figuratively speaking. After I find and catch Mocha, somebody could sneak over and open Marla's gate when she and Zero are asleep. Once the gate is open, Zero could roam free."

Christopher, the father of several small children, was not so sure. "As long as everyone else in town knows to stay inside for the duration. The rest of you wouldn't even be able to get in your cars and leave. We have a garage, but the rest of you don't."

All this talk about dogs and their various skills, proclivities, and personalities was fun, but it wasn't getting us anywhere. "So we let Zero roam while all the rest of us stay inside? I said. "Then the guy who appears with torn pants and tooth marks all over his legs is the bad guy?"

Helen shook her head. "I know you think we're all joking, 'Stel', but think about it. Each of us has skills that might help, too."

"You mean like Marla could sit on him," Bryce suggested with a smirk. Marla's excess weight, tendency to sweat profusely under stress, and inattention to personal hygiene made that thought unnerving.

"Or Nina could sweet talk him," Freda said.

In all fairness to Bryce, the rest of us should have seen this next idea coming and headed Bryce off at the pass. "Say," he said with a forehead slap. "I've just thought of something. What if I get my drone charged and send it out to patrol the neighborhood?" He pointed to the sky, then without waiting for a reply, he turned to go. "And you know what else? My dad could probably wire a gun to the drone! Then we'd have ourselves an armed patrol!"

"Hold the phone, Bryce!" I called, but he was already chugging away. I turned to the remaining neighbors. "Oh, that's perfectly dandy, a gun-wielding drone. Talk about your wild, wild west."

"He's planning to wire a gun to a drone?" Christopher said, watching Bryce disappear around the bend.

"Yes," said Helen. "And then while the drone is flying over us, the gun is going to come unwired, hit the ground, go off and shoot one of us fatally in the foot."

"Is there such a thing as a fatal shot to the foot" I said. "Although I guess a person could always bleed to death. Someone should go stop Bryce."

"What was that boy on about?" Freda asked. "A drone? That is something that flies?"

"Yes," Helen said, looking doubtful.

"It flies up there?" Freda pointed overhead. "And looks down on us and sees things?"

Helen and I glanced at each other. I took a stab at an explanation. "Well, it doesn't see, exactly. It has a camera on it, so it … shows a movie of what the camera is filming. Without film." Hmm. Explaining machines, especially semi-artifically intelligent machines, can be difficult. "It's like a movie camera mounted on a little flying machine."

"Oh," Freda said, nodding as though I was speaking in Spanish, a language which she does not understand. "And where do you go to see the movie?"

Finally, a question I knew the answer to. "Bryce's drone sends his movie to his computer monitor. That's what he uses to steer the drone. Or I guess nowadays he can use his phone, too."

"Oh." Freda was still nodding. "Let me see if I understand correctly. Bryce sits at home all night to watch his computer and tell his drone where to go and it takes a movie so we can see who is causing all this mischief?"

"Yep, that's about the size of it. Or his phone."

Helen brought us back to the previous topic. "And now he's headed home to wire a gun to his drone. I'm predicting a bad end to that. How's he gonna to aim and fire that gun?"

Good point, I thought.

Christopher had been following this conversation closely. "I don't know much about drones," he said, "but I don't think that's even possible."

"Especially not for a guy like Bryce?" I said.

"Right. I mean, obviously the military has drones that can aim at targets and drop explosives, but I don't think even they have airborne mechanical assassins."

A shiver went through me. Only a matter of time, I thought.

"Well, I certainly hope Bryce is not going to be dropping bombs on Arroyo Loco," Helen said. "Somebody should follow that fool home and stop him. Or at least remind him he's supposed to be sending out an email about the meeting."

Carefully avoiding eye contact, I said, "Good idea, Helen. Why don't you go do that?"

Not a half second later, Bryce appeared again, at a slow trot, head down. When he got close enough, he called out, "Anybody here know anyone who could lend me a gun?"

"No," I said, possibly more emphatically than strictly necessary.

Without lifting his head, Bryce made a u-turn and headed home again, possibly in a fit of pique that no one would offer him a firearm.

"Oh, dear," Freda said. "And in the meanwhile, I need to get busy on those cookies for the teenager patrol." Mumbling something to herself in German, she bustled homeward.

Helen leaned indecisively forward and back. I promised her I would set some time aside in the morning to help her look for Mocha, and suggested she could set some cat kibble inside the catio and hope Mocha returned on his own. She expressed confidence that some critter would definitely appreciate the offering, but was less sure than I that the critter who showed up to eat the kibble would be Mocha. She probably had a point.

The Friday night meeting turned out to be somewhat disjointed. About twelve of us assembled in our customary circle of folding chairs at the appointed hour. As president of the homeowners association, Graciela took her place standing in the center of the circle. No agreement had been reached about setting up a patrol, so those in attendance kept popping out of their chairs to go outside and try to catch a glimpse of their own house, or the road leading to their house, or the sky over their house, or something. After about the third such interruption, which included pretty much everyone stepping outside for a quick look around, Graciela retreated to a chair in the shadows outside the circle and sat fuming, her eyes narrowed in fury. Not getting the respect she felt she was entitled, I guess.

What with the car break-ins that had already happened, almost everyone had brought their cars to the roadhouse where parking was at a premium. I had a better excuse than most, since bringing my car gave me a good place to stow Shiner and Scout. They theoretically weren't allowed inside the roadhouse.

Bryce unfurled a large newsprint pad on an easel and called for a list of all of the acts of mischief that had already occurred. Before anyone had a chance to suggest anything, he wrote "stolen packages/porch pirates" at the top of the page. Maybe it was time to revoke Bryce's marking pen privileges if he was going to hijack the list. I still was not convinced any packages had gone missing in Arroyo Loco, although that darned replacement part I'd ordered for my blender was taking its own sweet time getting here. I opened my mouth to sputter my disagreement about listing the alleged porch thefts, then decided the argument wasn't worth the effort. While I prefer to get along with my neighbors, Bryce and I are never going to be best friends anyway.

I was sitting right next to the pad, and by the time he had added the spray paint at Graciela's house, a bicycle taken years ago from Delia's rear porch, the opened trunk and missing items from Grant's Buick, and the break in at Lauren's, I began to feel light-headed from the fumes of the marking pen.

"Don't you forget the thefts from my yard!" Freda said. "Twice now. Write that down, twice now."

"We need another list," Helen said. "Picking someone else's tomatoes may be mischief, but breaking into cars is more serious than mischief."

"And so is spraying paint," Graciela added in a tight voice.

"What would you call that then?" Bryce's writing hand wavered over the pad.

"Mayhem," Helen said. "Mayhem."

"Those are crimes," Graciela argued. "No reason to call them anything else. I've reported the paint to the sheriff. How would you like to have spray paint all over your house?"

Bryce flipped to a new page, wrote "crimes" at the top and moved the spray paint incident to that page. He also wrote "damage to Grant's Buick," on that page and added the vandalism and theft from Diego's new car.

"You know," I said in a tentative voice, "Grant broke that window himself when he backed out so fast."

"What's your point, Estela?" Bryce asked, lowering his brows.

I didn't want to get into the middle of an argument. On the other hand, didn't we already have enough actual mysterious events without overblowing the broken window on Grant's car? "Maybe it would be better to write about someone getting into and out of the trunk on Grant's Buick, and leave the broken window out of it?"

Bryce scratched away at his writing on the newsprint, crossing out a few words here, inserting one or two there and finished by writing "Grant's trunk" on the list. I was feeling downright woozy by then from the fumes, and got up to find a seat farther from the marking pen.

CHAPTER NINE

When I stood up to move to the other side of the circle, that started another stampede to the door, and then a general peering about the neighborhood. Between refilling coffee cups and visits to the facilities, it was easily another fifteen minutes before most of us got settled again and we got back to work.

"Don't forget Nina's house key being stolen from under her flowerpot," someone called out. Bryce dutifully added this item to the "mischief" list.

I added, "What about the things that are happening that are not much more than curious? Like someone de-cluttering the Rankins' yard and putting the toys away every night. Where does that go?" As I spoke, I stood and relieved Bryce of his first list. Helen grabbed a roll of tape from the office supply box where we keep pens and what not, and helped me attach the "mischief" list to the wall. We stuck the "crimes" list to the left of that, and a blank sheet with no title next to that. I scored myself an odorless red crayon and wrote on the blank page, "mysteries" then added "putting toys away" as the first item on that list.

"What about all that trash in the park?" Christopher asked. No one else had heard about that, so we had to take a few moments to listen to his complaints of finding food wrappers scattered on the ground near the lone picnic table yesterday morning.

"*Verdammit*, people are such pigs!" Freda said, suddenly and uncharacteristically furious. Those missing vegetables were still irking her.

I felt it necessary to point out that earlier this summer we had voted against supplying a trash container near the table in the park, so we shouldn't be too surprised if folks were leaving their trash on the ground. At the time we'd voted, no one had been willing to take responsibility for carrying a trash container to the dumpster every week to empty it. It was decided that those finding themselves in the park with litter to dispose of would need to pack said litter home. Apparently, either not everyone was living up to that commitment, or whoever had left the trash was not a voting member of the Arroyo Loco Homeowners Association.

"What kind of wrappers were they?" Nina said. "We could do some detecting and figure out who left those in the park." She raised her eyebrows at me and gave me an encouraging nod. Sometimes, when circumstances warrant, I do some consulting with Detective Muñoz and the county sheriffs. This hardly seemed like one of those circumstances.

A gravelly voice from across the room said, "They are the same wrappers from the diet bars stolen from my back porch." Marla Weisel appeared in the entryway. That was a surprise, as was the announcement that Marla would have in her possession a selection of diet bars. Or had at one time had such bars, which evidently now were missing and presumed, by her, to have been stolen.

"Hmm," I said. "So someone went onto your back porch, Marla? They stole the bars, and took them to the park to eat, where they then discarded the wrappers?"

Marla nodded slowly, her eyes narrow slits of fury in her round face. She was looking right at me. What? Did she think I had stolen her precious diet bars?

"How did the thief get on your porch?" I said. "I mean, where was Zero?" My question was followed by a roomful of mumbling agreement.

"It had to have been some time last night or the night before," Marla said. "When Zero and I would have been asleep."

Across the room, the coffee machine burbled. That's how quiet it was. We all sat imagining the bravery, or possibly desperate hunger, that would drive anyone to risk a trip onto Marla and Zero's back porch for a few diet bars. That had to have been the act of one famished individual. Either that, or someone with the unlikely history of having established rapport with Zero.

Helen leaned in close to me, elevating her eyebrows to their highest. She whispered in my ear. "Mocha?"

I tried to picture the giant coffee-and-cream colored long-furred cat creeping onto Marla's back porch, snagging a couple of diet bars, and carrying them to the picnic table to devour. I shook my head in doubt. "Anyway," I added, "Christopher said he found the wrappers yesterday morning and Mocha didn't go missing until today. So, no, I don't think so."

Bryce wandered over to the page labelled "mischief" and wrote "stolen diet bars, Marla's" as the next item on the list.

"And littering in the park," Christopher added. "Don't forget that."

"Humph, littering," Helen said. "Now we're being petty. Doesn't anyone have anything more serious to add to the list?"

"I'm not sure where this goes," Sunshine said, "but when I leave my rake or broom out front overnight, someone cleans my front walk. I've never seen who ... " She turned a questioning glance at Nina, who shrugged her innocence.

"Oh, yes," Freda said, "that happens at my house too, and sometimes they rake the leaves in the yard. I always thought it was Lauren helping me. I never did know why she raked at night, and I didn't ask her."

Since Lauren was not in attendance, we couldn't ask her either. I found myself wondering if I could get the same service by leaving the gate open to my rear yard and the pooper scooper in evidence. Probably no such luck, huh?

"Okay, so what have we got so far?" I stepped to the crimes list and read aloud. "For serious crimes we have, spray painting and vandalism on Graciela's house, breaking into or out of Grant's car ... "

"And stealing my golf club," Helen said. I added that to the list. Even one golf club can be astonishingly expensive.

I continued. "Breaking into and stealing from Diego's car. Breaking into Lauren's house." I stared at the list, then looked at those in the circle. "Anything else of a serious nature?"

Randy's mother, Catherine, timidly raised her hand. Graciela spun and fixed Catherine with an intimidating glare. "What?" she said.

"Um, well, I wanted to tell someone that Randy, you know, my son Randy? Well, he told me he saw someone getting out of Grant's trunk the other morning."

This elicited a more excited level of mumbling. At last, a break in the case, I thought. This could solve everything. We all turned interested faces to Catherine.

"Randy said he was on his way to ask DeVon, you know, Delia Jackson's son, DeVon?"

"Yes, yes," Helen said, rolling her hand in that get-on-with-it gesture.

Catherine turned a confused expression toward Helen, who dropped her hands into her lap. "Anyway," Catherine said, "Randy was on his way to ask DeVon about something and he said he saw someone getting in or out of the trunk of Grant's car. Or, at least, the car in front of your house, Helen."

"Catherine," I said, trying to gentle my tone. "Did Randy see who it was? And were they getting in the trunk, or out of it?"

"Yes," said Catherine.

"Yes? So who was it?"

"Or I mean no," Catherine said. "He didn't see who it was because it wasn't light yet. You know, this was before dawn. But the person was getting in and out. Or getting out and then in. You know, there's a tiny light inside car trunks? I don't know any more than that, really. You should ask Randy. He said he thought someone was hiding in the trunk of that big car. You know. Ask him. Oh, and by the way, someone got into our car, too, last night."

Questions erupted from various points in the circle. People wanted to know if windows had been broken, or anything stolen.

"No, no, the car was unlocked," Catherine said.

"Humph," Helen said. "Great, so now that's the solution? Leave all your cars unlocked so you don't have to make expensive repairs?"

Catherine waited with wide eyes, then said, "There was a box of cereal in there, those little 'o's, you know? And it's gone. I just figured the kids ate it. The cereal, I mean, not the box. I keep it in there for when Shawn gets to whining and I'm trying to drive."

We all stared silently at Catherine for another couple of seconds. Hard to know if a missing half-box of stale cereal really rose to the level of even mischief.

Bryce had been listening intently. He stood beside the lists, his arms crossed tightly, a look of increasing anger on his face. "I still think we need a gate, cameras, and a night patrol. What else has to happen before you people see the light?"

"Why does that sound like a threat, Bryce?" Helen tipped her head in his direction.

Hesitant to mention it, I said, "What happened with your drone? I thought you were going to patrol using the drone."

Bryce clenched his teeth in an angry scowl. "My dad wouldn't let me use it. He said we need a gate and cameras." We had reached an impasse, since we'd never approve either of those, or be able to afford them.

Helen had another thought. "You know, instead of a bunch of us wandering all over Arroyo Loco in the dark searching for the perpetrators of mischief and criminal activity, possibly Sunshine could be persuaded to bring to bear her psychic powers." Helen turned a confrontational face toward Sunshine.

Someone groaned quietly. Might have been me. Now was not really a good time for Helen to try to get on Sunshine's last nerve by provoking an argument about her alleged psychic powers, which, in all fairness to Helen, did seem to come and go in a somewhat willy-nilly fashion.

"I beg your pardon, Helen?" Sunshine turned her enigmatic smile in Helen's direction. Uh-oh. I hate it when Sunshine goes all enigmatic. It usually means she thinks the rest of us are bringing her down with negativity.

Helen forged ahead, explaining her suggestion again.

I could almost hear Sunshine's teeth grinding. "I'll see what I can do, Helen," was all she said, averting further ugliness.

Freda chose that moment to rush onto the porch and make another survey uphill. I was startled by how dark the canyon had become. This late in the summer, the days are already growing darker much earlier. I wasn't the only one who noticed.

"Okay, thank you everyone," Graciela said. "Let's wrap this up and get home. If anyone thinks of anything else that should go on the list, let me know."

The rest of us gathered our belongings, which didn't amount to much since the idea of bringing food to the meeting had sort of flopped. Thick billows of coastal fog shrouded the hills when we stepped outside, explaining the premature darkness. Late August is not the prime season for morning and evening fog, but it happens. When it rolls in, we are deprived of our long warm evenings suitable for porch-sitting, and those brilliant early mornings that lift even the most melancholy of hearts.

A few people made their way into the muddle of the haphazardly parked vehicles. A small clot of us stayed on the porch and watched as, one by one, the drivers disentangled their cars and head toward home.

Helen struggled to get one arm into her sweater. When the fog settles in, the temperature can drop by twenty degrees inside of an hour here in the canyon. "Who's going to talk to Randy?" she said. "Sounds like he might know something."

"I'll talk to him if I can find him," I volunteered. "But who can ever find him?"

"Chances are he doesn't know anything anyway," Bryce said. "Everybody always thinks Randy knows everything."

Hmm, I wondered, what's going on between Bryce and Randy? Those two were usually, but not always, chummy. Maybe Bryce was jealous that Randy seemed to be in on something Bryce wasn't.

"How do we know he even saw anyone getting into or out of the trunk?" Bryce said. "Probably he just saw someone messing near the back of Grant's car."

Helen frowned. "Why would someone be messing around there?"

Bryce was getting steamed again. He turned a reddening face on Helen. "How would I know? They could've been trying to tear off a bumper sticker or something. Grant's probably one of those guys ... he's probably one of those guys that has that national rifle group's bumper stickers or something."

Bad timing. Graciela appeared in the open doorway, pulled it closed, and gave us her back while she locked it. She turned slowly to face us. "Oh, for pity's sake. If you aren't the most annoying, blind-to-the-ways-of-the-world bunch of people I've ever met. I don't know what all."

"Don't start in on us," Helen said. "You're the one with the backwoods mentality."

"Backwoods!"

I put a gentle hand on Graciela's shoulder. "Easy, easy, let's chill here. I know we have some differences of opinion, but right now we're all on edge. Let's don't take it out on each other."

Graciela pursed her lips in a disgusted pout, shook off my hand, and stomped down the steps toward her front door on the other side of the road.

"Can you give me a lift, 'Stel'?" Helen said. "The sheriff impounded our one car yesterday, you know. They said the trunk might have evidence in it, or on it. Freda had to give me a ride to go pick up Grant last night, and he caught a lift into town this morning with Nina. He's supposed to stop and get a rental after work tonight. What a headache! Can they keep your car forever, just because someone else might have used it to commit a crime? Grant's pretty sure our insurance won't cover the cost of the rental, so we're stuck … "

She continued in this vein even after I'd driven her to her driveway, and was stepping out. I don't think I got more than an occasional "Hmm," in during the entire trip.

It was not until I'd dropped Helen off that I really saw the swirling fog deepening the darkness surrounding me. I hit the lock button on all five doors to the Subaru. My headlamps caught drifts of fog. Droplets of moisture trickled at the edges of my vision, catching sparkles of faint light as they slid down the windshield. Shadowy shapes seemed to slip along the side of the car nearest the canyon drop-off, and then just as quickly, disappear. I focused on the feeble streetlamp ahead, but when I got under it, even more phantoms twisted in the reflected fog beneath that light. It did not help that both dogs stood peering out the windows as though they too were seeing ghosts surrounding us.

Still feeling off-center, and not yet used to my recently narrowed driveway, I nearly veered into my new, half-planted garden. Correcting at the last minute, we rolled into the driveway and stopped in the sudden glare of the motion-detector flood lamp. I turned the engine off and gazed around us. Briefly wondered if maybe we should try sleeping in the car. Thought about Diego's car window smashed the night before, and decided to chance going on inside. After all, I wasn't alone. I had my dogs.

Casting caution to the wind, together we scurried onto the porch and inside. I threw the deadbolt behind us and stood there watching the dogs. As usual, Scout went immediately to check his food bowl on the off-chance someone had left something unexpected there. Shiner waited nearby, then moved in for a long drink of water. After a good ninety-seconds of steady slurping, he plopped on his bed in the living room. Neither dog seemed remotely alarmed at anything inside the house.

I double-checked all the window latches. What else? Realized I had left the porch door unlocked again. Not only that, but those dogs were going to need to hit the backyard one more time before we could go to bed.

It's always a dilemma. Do you turn on every light you own and thus give the bad guys all the light they need to commit their nefarious attacks? Or do you turn off the lights and make them trips over things and stumble around in the dark?

I decided I had a few more moments of bravery in me, so I called the dogs, flipped every outside light on, and we all stepped onto the porch again. The dogs went through their door to the yard while I latched the screened door and did a quick inventory of the small refrigerator so I'd know in the morning if we'd suffered another loss. All that remained was a box of baking soda quietly absorbing odors from no food. Quick inventory.

The dogs popped back through their door and I took their word for it they had done everything that would need doing before dawn. Unless someone was ill, they always let me sleep until the sun has well and truly arisen and the bad guys had finished creeping through the darkness.

We settled into bed, me with a slightly scary book, and after just a few moments there was a distant boom outside and the power went out. Probably another drunk driver on the highway had taken that turn before Arroyo Loco Road a tad too tightly and side-swiped the transformer box on the shoulder. Wouldn't be the first time that had happened, and there wasn't a thing to do about it. Doubtless several of my more easily annoyed neighbors had already called in the outage. All I could do was roll over and go to sleep, which I resolved to do.

I got the pillows arranged to my satisfaction, pulled the covers to my chin, and promptly set about worrying. Did I know if this outage effected the whole town? Maybe my house was the only one without power. Should I call someone else? I lifted the handset for my landline, but without electricity, all I got out of it was dead silence. I keep a rotary phone under my bed for exactly these kinds of emergencies, but I didn't think anyone else in town had one. Even if I dug it out and tried to call, no one else would answer. Just for the heck of it, I tried. When I got it plugged in, the phone gave off with a reassuring dial tone. I dialed Nina's number, then listened to it ring and ring. No answer. I went back to worrying.

A few more minutes of that, and I remembered I lived in the twenty-first century, as did my neighbors, and most of us have mobile phones. As long as their charges held, we could use those devices to communicate.

Gently, I slapped the top of my nightstand until I located my mobile phone, then sent a quick text to Helen.
Is your power out?

Her response beeped back a few seconds later.
Yes power is out power co says back on in two hours. I'm busy

Well, pardon me, I thought, and disconnected. At least now I knew the power outage wasn't only at my house. I rolled over and tried again, without success, to sleep.

CHAPTER TEN

Ten-thirty. The power was still out, and I was yet to fall asleep. Maybe, I thought, the dogs and I should go spend the night somewhere else. Somewhere with light and other people. Maybe Amanita had had the right idea by leaving. But where would I go?

My boss Veneta would probably take us in. The nice thing about working with a bunch of psychotherapists is they are usually understanding when an emergency arises and you need help. Then again, I don't know Veneta all that well. Anyway, Veneta is my neighbor Delia Jackson's sister, so even if Veneta had extra room at her house, she'd probably already taken in Delia and her kids. The Jacksons' house is between mine and Helen's, so if the power is out here and at Helen's, it's surely also out at Delia's. My thoughts kept going in circles.

Maybe we could go stay at the sheep ranch that doubles as our dog day care during the school year. Inez Gabiola's ranch house isn't large, but it might fit us. She already squeezes in her own border collies at night. Then I remembered that Inez had recently married. That might be awkward. She might suggest we sleep in the barn, which would hardly be an improvement over my own bed in the dark with a potential bad guy or guys roaming somewhere outside.

Needless to say, I wasn't getting much sleep. I flipped over and punched my pillow into submission again. About then Shiner decided he'd had enough. He stood, shook himself, and headed for the usually forbidden couch in the living room. Scout tried to follow his brother, but I was not sleeping in that bedroom alone. I ordered Scout to "go to bed" He grumbled, but curled again in his dog bed.

Maybe we could stay with Nina? She had all those nice new locks. I tried to imagine two medium-sized black and white shedding and sometimes muddy border collies sleeping in Nina's impeccably decorated home. That seemed unlikely to go well.

Maybe we could invite Nina to stay here with us? I must have drifted off at some point or that idea would never have occurred to me. Nina had been inside our cozy home for dinner once or twice. I remember she threatened to redecorate the place, starting with reopening my permanently nailed shut front door with the porch outside barely hanging onto the wall. Nina thought I should create a welcoming entry walkway leading from the driveway to the front door, instead of having all my guests enter through the scruffy screened porch and directly into the kitchen.

No, having Nina here would not work out. I like my house the way it is, with all its flaws. Besides, I've always thought welcoming visitors directly into the kitchen added to the warmth and friendliness of the place. Nina's house is nice, but it always feels a bit stiff and formal.

Another loud bump brought me alert in a flash. That one sounded closer, like maybe on the side of the house. It was followed by silence. Should I go check, or hope that was the last of it? There wasn't a word from Shiner, who presumably was sleeping on the couch in the living room. The red numerals on my bedside clock read ten fifty. Not that late. I picked up the phone again and found Nina's number. How I would get myself, and the dogs, safely out to the car and over to Nina's, I did not know. Cross that bridge when I got to it.

Nina was laughing when she answered my call.

"What's so funny?" I said. Then I heard more laughter in the background. As it turned out, Nina had freaked when the power first went off and bugged out to a coworker's place in town, where they were proceeding to have a wine-fueled laugh-fest. Feeling left out, I grumbled.

Nina tried to console me. "I know you think the thefts in Arroyo Loco are someone else, a prison escapee or someone else, Estela, but I am convinced it's Martin, my daughter's former boyfriend. He threatened to get me once, punish me for making Angela break up with him. I had to get out of there. Why don't you come here?"

Nina was sincere, but she meant me, not me and my two dogs, so ixnay on that idea. I suddenly felt lonesome, standing there clinging to a tiny voice coming through the plastic device in my hand. "I need to disconnect now. Don't want to run the battery down." I assured Nina I was fine and told her to have fun.

I tiptoed to the living room and found Shiner sound asleep on the couch. If there was something going on outside our house, it was not anything that worried the dog. I went back to bed, cracked open the blind, and tried to read by moonlight until sometime much later, when I fell asleep drooling on my book.

Saturday morning started a lot earlier than usual. With a "bzzt," the power came back on at about six, along with the lamp on my nightstand. I switched that glare off and was just snuggling down again when my phone jangled next to my head where I had left it the night before. Bleary-eyed I peered at the display. Couldn't read it, and didn't feel like coming awake enough to search for my reading glasses. Decided whoever it was could leave a message and I would listen to that when the real morning arrived.

This was followed shortly by banging on my porch door. Well, shoot. This was making me mad. Sure, there probably was some fresh crisis in Arroyo Loco, but why did it have to involve me? Unless the canyon was on fire. This was late August, prime fire season in California. Maybe the canyon was on fire. I pulled on my bathrobe and headed for the door. The canyon better be on fire.

Bryce had already started off down the hill by the time I yanked the door open and stuck my head out.

He turned back when he heard the door squeal. "Emergency at the roadhouse, Estela! All hands on deck for this one!"

"Bryce, stop!" To my surprise, he did. "Come back here." And again, he did, although with some reluctance. "What emergency, Bryce?" He even had the audacity to look somewhat chagrined. Apparently the canyon was not on fire.

"Raymond called," he said. "Someone tried to pry open our mailboxes. They got into a couple of them."

I'm sure the expression on my face told him how important I thought this latest crisis was in the larger scheme of things. And by "larger scheme" I meant specifically in the scheme of how much restful sleep I generally need in order to present myself as halfway human.

Bryce looked away, then back at me. "It's a federal crime, Estela. Breaking into mailboxes is a federal crime. We have to call the feds."

"Good, Bryce, you go do that, and in the meantime, leave me out of it." I slammed the door. "Honestly," I muttered, then slid open the panel, letting the dogs out.

No point in going back to bed, I took a shower. By the time I was out with my wet hair partially styled, there were two more messages on my phone. Both announcing that the usual Saturday morning coffee klatch at the roadhouse would be expanded to a community-wide gathering for the purpose of discussing the mailbox caper.

Usually, the most appealing thing about the Saturday morning coffee-klatch was that the homeowners association sprang for the pastries, and they came from a real bakery in one of the nearby towns. I rarely find the pastries appealing enough to overcome my reluctance to join the idle chatter of a neighborhood gossip and gab-fest, but decided I should probably at least go find out what the deal was with the mailboxes. I leashed the dogs and poured a second cup of coffee into my handy to-go cup. The pastries might be worth stopping for, but it is best to avoid the coffee at all costs.

As I stepped off the porch, a blood-curdling scream interrupted the otherwise mostly peaceful morning. This was followed immediately by more screams, different voices, and some general hollering. Then another scream, and someone yelling "Run! Run! Oh, God, run!" A door slammed.

Hmm. Out of an abundance of caution, I popped both dogs back inside the kitchen and closed their dog door opening. I carefully shut the screened porch door. Briefly thought about also locking the latch on that door, but decided the baking soda in the small refrigerator could fend for itself for a bit. Peering as far down the road as I could, all I saw was a normal summer morning, although now eerily quiet. Hmm. I went back to the porch and fished my new binoculars out of their basket. I focused. Still nothing, and the screams had gone silent. I tipped my to-go cup and took a sip of coffee.

There was nothing for it except to go see what all the excitement had been about. When I reached the curve in the road and could see a few of my neighbor's homes, the scene reminded me of that Twilight Zone episode where the whole town has been abandoned. From an upstairs window at Lauren's house, a young woman I didn't recognize gave me a tentative finger wave. Everyone else had vanished. I continued downhill, tiptoed across the bridge, and paused there to assess the situation.

I could see the single-engine garage where we store our leaky old fire engine to my right, and across the road, the overgrown weeds around the falling down house where Thomas and Margaret used to live. I could also see the front yard of Marla's house. I scanned again. Something wasn't right.

I stared longer and slowly it dawned on me that the gate in Marla's front picket fence was off its hinges. Someone had removed the gate and leaned it against the fence, leaving a gaping hole. What was worse, Marla's front door stood slightly ajar. My next thought was obvious. Where was Zero, Marla's vicious dog? I crept farther down the road, staying on the opposite side from Marla's. I got to a place where I could see the rest of Arroyo Loco.

Nina stood on her porch, well behind her own fence. Others crowded behind her. More people milled on Sunshine and Raymond's porch also, the house door open and several folks poised to dash inside. Everyone was uncharacteristically quiet. Across the road, a cluster of small faces peered out from Christopher and Jessica's front window. Nina caught sight of me, and her hand went to her mouth. She gestured frantically to get away. I was backed against Catherine's hedge and didn't have much in the way of an escape route. Not to mention, at that point I wasn't one hundred percent sure what the danger might be, or from what direction it might be coming.

Something moved on the ground in my near vision, maybe about twenty feet away. I focused in on a badly damaged pink bakery box. And next to it, calmly licking the remains of whatever had been inside, was Zero, Marla's man-eating basenji. Having demolished our tasty coffee klatch pastries, the dog drooled and gazed speculatively in my direction. Up on the porch, Freda moaned loudly. I hoped she was mourning the loss of the pastries, not grieving over my imminent demise, which at that moment appeared all but certain.

Heavy breathing bore down on me from behind. I didn't want to make any sudden moves that might startle the basenji.

I waited until the breathing was almost upon me before I risked a slow head turn. Marla headed this way, wearing a disgusted expression and carrying a leather leash.

"Honestly, you people!" she said, as though the humans had brought this situation on themselves. Which I guess might not be entirely out of the question. You know what they say about how dogs can smell fear? Given what all else dogs can smell, I wouldn't be a bit surprised if a whole community of humans screaming and racing for nearby porches might be easily sensed by your random average dog. And who can blame a dog for eating pastries that get lost in the general shuffle and land on the ground nearby? Really, the whole situation was entirely understandable.

I was on the verge of a sigh of relief at the appearance of the dog owner when a low growl arrested my attention. I eased my head forward again, and made eye contact with the basenji, who was clearly contemplating my throbbing jugular hungrily. I tried hard not to whimper.

"Come here you stupid mutt," Marla said. I had to admire her bravado. Basenjis are smallish dogs, but I'd lost track of how many folks Zero had already bitten in his short life, one of them being his own loving companion, Marla, and she had the scars on her hand to prove it. She held the leash's clasp in front of the dog and continued to bravely approach. He snapped and she jerked back, almost knocking me into the hedge. Thank goodness the ditch that used to be there had been piped underground.

Snapping again and snarling angrily, Zero lunged toward Marla's leg, his white fangs flashing in the morning sun. Screaming, Marla kicked at the dog and made a mad dash for

Raymond's porch, Zero in hot pursuit. Arms reached out to help drag Marla to safety, punctuated by a ripping sound as Zero leapt upwards and tore a sizable piece out of his owner's skirt. In a flash, all the humans disappeared inside and the door slammed, leaving Zero alone, pacing at the porch steps. He turned and looked at me again.

I glanced to all sides, not liking my odds. My nearest possible sanctuary was across the road at Christopher's house. Far enough away that no matter how fast I dashed, Zero could get a flying leap of a head start off those porch steps and easily catch up to me. Plus, I had a disturbing lack of confidence that Christopher and Jessica would admit me even if I were lucky enough to get to their front door before being reduced to Zero's new bloody chew toy. I didn't move, barely breathing.

Zero conceded his post near the porch and ambled back in the direction of the bakery box and my shins. Raymond's door creaked open and he emerged, although it took me a moment to recognize him. The late summer morning was already hot, but Raymond wore long heavy jeans, work boots, a thick denim jacket and leather work gloves. A woolen scarf encircled his neck and was tucked into the jacket's collar. He clunked down the steps carrying Zero's leash and came resolutely forward.

He didn't stop, but as he neared he tossed a wad of mystery meat onto the ground in front of the dog. Zero lunged for the meat. Deftly, Raymond slipped the leash under the back of Zero's collar and jerked it tight. One of his heavy gloves fell off in the process, and it took Raymond a couple of seconds of terrified fumbling to pull it back on. Zero went crazy, snarling and snapping at Raymond's legs and attempting to sink his teeth into the work boots.

Marla stumbled coming out the door. Someone may have even pushed her. She hurried out to the road and grabbed the leash. This did not serve to disengage Raymond since Zero had his teeth firmly clamped onto Raymond's jacket. The strange tableau made up of the round woman in half a skirt and the tall bundled man with a snarling dog hanging off his denim sleeve, made its way to Marla's house and disappeared inside. As he came back our way, Raymond propped Marla's gate back in place and latched it. That wouldn't hold for long, but it was better than nothing.

I took the opportunity to scamper inside Nina's front gate, then we waited. Those of us who had lived in Arroyo Loco long enough, knew to wait and make sure Zero didn't go in his front door and immediately come popping back out the kitchen door.

Freda was still moaning in despair and gazing at the demolished bakery box. Helen patted her hand. "Never mind, Freda," she said. "I have some Entemann's in my freezer. I can go get that."

"Ooh, yes," Freda said, "I have a *gugelhupf* I can bring also."

"Come on gals," Nina said, lifting her car keys from the ring by her door. "Let's go get those goodies."

After Nina's new Lexus rolled out in pursuit of replacement pastries, a few of us gathered in her front yard behind the fence. We were trying to decide if enough time had elapsed to make a crossing to the roadhouse prudent when a ruckus erupted across the road at Christopher and Jessica's house. Three small boys spilled down the steps and toward the minivan, all dressed in adorable blue and yellow soccer uniforms, each in a successively smaller size. Jessica tugged a fourth boy, just a toddler, by the hand and carried the baby in her arms. The whole family piled into the vehicle. This was followed by much ado buckling into car seats and seat belts. The van backed out and disappeared out onto the highway. I guess young families don't really have time for the regular Saturday morning coffee klatch and gossip session that the rest of us were about to enjoy.

CHAPTER ELEVEN

We got busy placing tables and chairs in the sun on the roadhouse porch. The ladies returned with the baked goods and Helen went to work getting the coffeepot going. A couple of folks gathered in front of the mangled mailboxes. Keeping my priorities straight, I leaned in to Nina and whispered.

"What's a google-huff?"

"*Gugelhupf,*" she said, getting the accent perfect. "I believe it's a kind of bundt cake."

I nodded slowly, not entirely sure I knew what a bundt cake was either, but not wanting to appear uneducated. Not that it mattered anyway. I'm reasonably adventurous when it comes to sweets and was willing to try anything once.

Most people had disappeared inside the building and from the sound of it, there was quite a commotion going on in there. A stack of paper plates and plastic forks sat on a folding card table on the porch. I sidled in that direction, not seeing any point in getting involved in whatever was going on inside. I was almost forced to rethink my position when Amanita's car rolled into the lot, coming from the direction of town. Guess she was not about to miss a chance to gossip with her neighbors, even though she had abandoned the neighborhood in its hour of need. I thought about scurrying inside with the others before Amanita arrived on the porch, but it sounded as though they were on their way out anyway.

Sure enough, the rest of the crowd emerged seconds later, uttering no end of expletives that would have to be deleted from any family oriented publication. It seemed that not only had three of our mailboxes on the front porch been roughly pried open, but the window into the kitchen had also been smashed and glass scattered everywhere.

After an earlier incident in that kitchen, we no longer stored or prepared food there, so although the cupboards had been opened and the contents of drawers scattered about, whoever had broken in had not netted much in the way of edibles. Our invader had vented his or her disappointment by dumping the ubiquitous box of baking soda, the only contents of the refrigerator, onto the middle of the linoleum, and upending the drawer of serving utensils on top of that. According to one eyewitness, an entire roll of waxed paper now festooned the countertops and floor. I elected not to view the destruction.

If you choose a seat early at one of these get-togethers, there is no telling who you might end up sitting next to, and having to listen to, for the subsequent hour or so. I chose to meander a bit, my coffee and cheese Danish in hand, before settling.

I checked out the bent mailboxes. Whoever had done that had had a heck a time getting them open, and had succeeded in prying only one corner down on each. The edge of a ripped envelope poked out of one, but it was unclear whether the culprit had been able to fully extract anything out of even that one.

Next to me, Sunshine Rainbow tut-tutted. "Why must some people behave like this? I just don't see why we can't all get along. Do you suppose one of our neighbors simply forgot to bring her mailbox key? I would gladly have lent her mine." It had recently become common knowledge that any one of our mailbox keys would work equally well in almost any of the mailboxes.

I pointed out that if the culprit had been another neighbor trying to access her own mail without use of a key, she, he, or they would not have pried open three different mailboxes.

"And look," Nina said, gesturing, "they broke off knife blades or something trying to get in." I got close. Sure enough, thin blades of broken-off metal were visible along the edges of one box.

"Betcha that's why they broke into the kitchen," Helen said. "They rifled through the silverware drawer to get knives."

"These mailboxes must be really hard to get into, " I said, marveling at the efforts we had expended to protect the armloads of junk mail we pulled out of those boxes and dumped into the waiting garbage can every day. "It looks like anything thin enough to wedge into those cracks was too thin to be of much help in prying. They all broke off." I looked at the floor, and sure enough, two broken off knife handles had been kicked to the side along with the rest of the usual detritus tracked onto the porch.

Raymond stood next to Sunshine, stripped down to his usual cargo shorts and worn polo shirt. He stared at the boxes, squinting, and scratching his frizzy graying hair. "What's puzzling me is, why these particular boxes?" he said. "I mean, why this box?" He stabbed a finger at box 601, "And not this one, box 602? Anyone know who belongs to box 601?"

"That is Lauren's box," Freda called from her seat at the far end of the tables. Folks were starting to claim chairs. I edged in Freda's direction, but Alice dashed over and slid into my intended destination before I could get there. Alice is harmless, but it can be challenging to carry on much of a conversation with her. She nods and smiles a lot, and says, "yes, yes," whenever she's spoken to. I'm never entirely sure she's all there.

"We take turns to bring each other's mail. That is how I know that is Lauren's box," Freda continued. "She gets her checks in the mail. She likes to get those collected quickly."

Lauren works at home in her upstairs office doing some kind of free-lance editing. Technical journals, I think. Makes sense that she would receive payments through the mail.

"Humph," Raymond said. "You suppose that's why this one was chosen? Someone hoping to find a check inside?"

"You know," I said, "these days it's really hard to kite a stolen check." Thought I'd throw in that tidbit of information. Long story how I know that. What I got for my trouble was a small chorus of blank stares.

Nina had a more pertinent thought. "How would anyone except Lauren," she turned her gaze on Freda, "or apparently Freda, know that was Lauren's box? You didn't know, Raymond."

"True," he said. No one else had a better answer. "So, why was that box chosen?"

"Well, duh," Helen said. "Look. All three of the pried open mailboxes are along the top. Guy was going for the low-hanging fruit. He must've thought the top boxes would be the easiest to get into."

We could all see that what Helen said was true. "And you know," I said, "he probably broke into the kitchen to get at the knives."

Helen lowered her brow at me. "Didn't I just now say that?"

"Oh, sorry. Yes, I guess you did."

At the other end of the tables, Bryce popped up, indignant with his hands on his hips. "How do you know it was a guy?"

I nodded my conciliation. "You're right, Bryce. I don't. Sorry. Sorry, everyone." I wasn't going to make much of a consultant to the sheriff's department if I kept making assumptions like that one.

At that point, Graciela arrived on the scene. Grim-faced, she glanced at the damaged mailboxes, then went inside to survey the wreckage there. The rest of us watched in silence. At least her gun was nowhere in evidence.

"Whoever it was," Raymond said, "I think we'd best call the sheriff."

"No!" Bryce said. "Not the county sheriff! This is a federal crime. We have to call the feds!"

"Who do you mean by 'the feds'," Nina said. "The FBI? Or one of those investigative agencies like on television?"

"Yes, yes," Alice said. "NCIS, you mean?" Her first contribution to the conversation.

"Well, not naval, but ... P-O-C-I-S? Post Office Criminal Investigative Services?" Bryce suggested.

"Poke-us?" came from somewhere at the other end of the table.

Nina rolled her eyes and shook her head at the same time. "Never mind."

"Might be best to wait for Walt to get here and ask him," Raymond said, referring to our regular mail delivery person. "I'll keep an eye on the situation until he gets here. In the meantime," he glared at Bryce, "I'll call the sheriff about that broken window in back. Could be some evidence with that."

"Looked to me like someone pitched that big rock through the window," Helen said. "It's hard to see how there would be too many fingerprints on a rock."

I licked the remains of my cheese danish from my fingers and contemplated an excuse to leave while my neighbors continued batting about theories as what had happened to our communal mailboxes.

Graciela chose that moment to emerge from the interior, as grim-faced as when she went inside. She narrowed her eyes and gazed slowly at each of us until everyone at the tables was silent. "I know some of you are willing to risk all our lives to protect your precious principles," she said, "but this has gone too far. Doing as Muñoz suggested and 'keeping an eye out' is not working. Every day something more serious happens, and the authorities still have not caught that violent criminal who escaped from the prison. We no longer have a choice. We must hire armed guards or go on risking our lives."

Silence reigned as we cut looks to one another. Who was going to stand up to Graciela? Naturally, it was Helen who spoke first.

"Criminy, Graciela, where are we getting the money for that? You yourself said the HOA treasury empties out faster than it fills up, with payments for the new bridge and sidewalks and all. We don't have any money for guards, armed or otherwise."

Graciela wasn't giving an inch. "If the homeowners won't vote to pay for armed guards, as president of the HOA, I will issue an executive order."

"Oh, get off it, Graciela. This isn't the White House." Helen stood and pulled herself to her full and quite intimidating height. "You can't do whatever you want no matter what the rest of us think. We pay our taxes ... er, our HOA dues, and that makes us the deciders, not you."

"We'll just see about that." Graciela glowered at Helen, going toe to toe with the larger woman. Both were turning nasty shades of purple.

Raymond stepped forward, although keeping far enough back that if fists started flying he would still be out of range. "Here now, let's all try to stay calm." Several of us eased backward, edging toward our nearest escape routes. "What happened to these mailboxes here, this is indeed a serious crime, but the authorities will take care of the investigation and repair. This is not our issue. And remember, Graciela, that paint job on your house happened long before any prisoner went missing. Other than that, I think Freda's missing tomatoes were the only mysterious happening we had going on here before that."

"And the packages stolen off porches," Bryce added. "That was before."

"And the key missing from under Nina's flowerpot," Helen said.

I thought about mentioning the mystery of the Rankins' toys being placed on their porch, also happening before this week, but left that unsaid. I was still hoping to make a discreet escape from the scene.

Graciela quivered in her fury, then stomped off the porch without saying another word. I kind of wish fewer people would stomp angrily down those old wooden porch steps. Those treads get a lot of traffic, and they're not going to last forever under that kind of abuse.

With that bit of ugliness over, the rest of us relaxed, and a few even settled in again to chat and finish off the pastries, which were universally judged as being as delicious as anything that might have been inside that demolished bakery box.

"Seriously," Nina said, "You know what we should get? We should get one of those fancy coffeemakers with the little pods you pop in."

"Ooh, yes," Freda agreed. "And each person can make whichever flavor they would like. Hazlenut, or French Vanilla, or whichever. That is a very good idea."

Helen nodded her agreement. "Beats battling with that ancient twenty-cup machine, that's for sure. We should ask Marla if we have enough money in petty cash. What does one of those things cost, anyway?"

"Someone should look into that," Nina said, making eye contact with those present. Almost everyone chose that moment to take another sip of their own coffee, become absorbed in picking the crumbs off their paper napkins, or gaze absently into space off to their left.

When the conversation resumed, it was mostly about who might be committing what seemed like random acts of mischief, and where they might be hiding.

"Now we need to revise our list," Bryce said. "You know, of the crimes. What they were, when they were committed. We should call another meeting."

Keeping our list current was a good idea, no question about that. His idea ran off the rails at that point, as far as I was concerned. Sure, two heads are sometimes better than one, but more often than not, trying to complete any task at one of our homeowners meetings was doomed to dissolve into verbal chaos.

"How about if I add the mailboxes to the list," I said. "Then it will be there next time we want to have a discussion. What exactly did you want added?"

"Well, duh, Estela," Bryce said, garnering my undying affection. "The mailboxes?"

"Yes, of course, the mailboxes."

"And what about the broken window in the kitchen?" Nina said. "Is that a crime or just mayhem?"

"You'd call it a crime if you were the one who was going to get stuck boarding it up," Bryce said.

From there, the conversation drifted to questions about where the inmate might be hiding, or if, in fact, he was anywhere near Arroyo Loco. Several of us expressed doubt that this might be the case, but the younger and more energetic among us were eager to search anyway.

Bryce had another one of his bright ideas. "The one place that makes the most sense for a bad guy to be hiding out is in that big house."

He referred to the new, but long vacant McMansion at the far end of Arroyo Loco Road, on top of the hill. The house has been tied up in litigation for over a year, and was securely locked, all the windows sealed with plywood, and a cyclone-type fence encircling the entire structure. Last time my dogs and I walked past, there was even a closed-circuit security camera scanning the front of the house.

"How could someone have gotten inside there without setting off those alarms?" Raymond asked.

"Exactly," I said. "And anyway, Muñoz and his deputies searched that house along with all the others when they were here."

"They didn't even go inside the fence," Bryce said. "I was right there watching them. All they did was walk around outside the fence, and make sure the padlock was still on there. They didn't even think the escapee was here in Arroyo Loco two days ago. They still thought he was at the prison. I'm telling you, they did not conduct a serious search. Now we know for a fact someone is here, doing stuff. I'll betcha anything that guy is hiding in that house. We should search it ourselves." Bryce stood and tugged his napkin from where it was tucked into his tee shirt. "Come on! Who's going with me?"

Arriving at that moment, Randy and other kids were up for anything, especially since our smaller-than-usual selection of pastries had almost all been consumed. "I'll go!" Randy said, as he and DeVon scooped the remaining three bear claws. DeVon handed his extra one to Sofia, and the three thundered down the steps.

"I'd like to go," Ernie said, attempting to maneuver his wheel chair out from under the table and in the direction of the ramp. "I've never seen the inside of that place. Bryce, give me a hand here, son."

Bryce had already started, but turned back and got behind his father's wheelchair. They made an initial head-start, what with the momentum from rolling down the ramp. From there it was all up hill. Bryce did his best to keep pace with the younger crowd, but it was slow-going pushing that chair. "Come on, Mom," he yelled back to Alice, his mother. "I'll drop you at home."

Amanita had the grace to look embarrassed for a moment before she offered to "take notes and make a report" and dashed off, trailing Bryce.

"Well, what the heck," Helen said, always game for an adventure. "Come on the rest of you. Somebody should keep an eye on those kids."

Only Freda joined her in bringing up the rear. Arms pumping, the two women gave it their all, trying to stay with the crowd.

Raymond stared glumly at the damaged mailboxes. "They're not even going to get inside the fence. That place is sealed tight." He shook his head. "I need a nap." He shambled down the ramp and off toward home.

That left Nina, Sunshine, and me to clean the tables. We put the chairs back inside, but decided we'd leave the tables for our more burly neighbors. I had enough work ahead of me planting the rest of my new garden without wasting energy putting away six-foot tables.

"Well shoot," Nina said. "Raymond is probably right. That *casa grande* is nothing but an attractive nuisance. We should either have it bull-dozed or move a nice family in there."

With a determined look, Sunshine was scrubbing at one of the tables. A persistent red spot there was not coming off. She sighed. "It's not really our problem, is it? I mean, isn't that place still tied up in court?"

"Yes, for more than a year now," I said. "What a waste." I shared the conviction that nothing of any interest would be found in the big house. If there had been anything to find there, surely Muñoz and his deputies would have found it. "I'm going home to plant my garden."

I got two of the ceanothus plants in before I broke for my mid-day meal. There were still a frightening number of plants sitting in their temporary pots at the edge of the garden, and I was anxious about getting their feet into the soil. I may have been over-generous with the soil amendments and worm-castings I was dumping into each hole, as it was beginning to look as though I might have to make another trip to the garden store in town to replenish my supplies.

I stood, stretched, and arched my now-aching back. Should I make that trip to town into an excuse to pick up some lunch prepared by someone other than me, and leave the planting for later?

CHAPTER TWELVE

As I broke from my toils, the neighbors who had raced to the big house, now a dejected band of would-be criminal capturers, trickled past, heading home. They had not found anything or anyone at the big house. What's more, they had not been able to find even one opening through the fence. Helen summed the situation up with, "Gadzooks! That house is fenced in and locked as tight as a chastity belt on a virgin."

After the chuckling died down, I pointed out that if the actual prison had been as securely locked as was that big house, the dangerous criminal would never have escaped in the first place.

Later that afternoon, I was back out front putting in the coral bells when Bryce rolled slowly past in his battered pickup. His rescue dog Tippy smiled and wagged at me, her head out the window on the passenger side.

"Hey! Estela!"

Sorely tempted to yell back, 'Hay is for horses, Bryce!' as my father would have done, I waved instead, but his wheels had stopped rolling. I lurched off my knees where I had been performing the ritual drenching with sea-weed extract, as I did with each new planting. "What?" I said. My sarcasm would have been wasted on Bryce anyway.

"The sheriff is here, Estela. The real sheriff, not one of his deputies. He's here with a United States Postal Service postal inspector. On a Saturday!"

I tried, but failed to be impressed. "Huh. Okay, well, have fun with that."

"Oh, I'm going to nail plywood over that kitchen window in back. Gonna reuse that plywood from when Nina's window got broken. That's why I have to take the truck. Have to take my tools." I gave him a wave that probably more closely resembled a brush-off, and bent again to the next plant.

I had been so industrious with my gardening that the only plants left yet to be put in the ground were the four emerald carpet manzanita ground covers. Those would need to wait, as I had indeed run out of worm-castings. I surveyed my work. The area was really shaping up. In a year or two, it would be thick with bird- and bug-friendly greenery, flowers, and berries. That is, it would be if the boar, gophers, voles, and human criminal element would leave it in peace long enough to become established. All of those critters are notorious for uprooting new plantings.

I used the rake to smooth out the ground at the base of each new plant, and gave special care to the ground surrounding the bird bath. I backed carefully away, leaving rake marks in the dirt. That way, if anything or anyone disturbed my new garden, or came to tip over the bird bath again, I would have a record of the paw/foot/shoe prints in the dirt. Carefully, I stowed the rake inside the shed in my locked backyard where a human would not be able to use it to erase their tracks.

From the porch steps, I appreciated my new garden. Sure, it looked sparse now, as I'd left plenty of room for each plant to grow and fill in, but someday it would be lush and filled with life. I had finally put down some actual roots in Arroyo Loco, approved or not.

I washed my hands, leashed the dogs, and got ready to walk to the roadhouse. Might as well see what was up, and in any case, I had to collect my mail. Glanced into the refrigerator and realized there was nothing in there for dinner except a half dozen eggs. I make do with scrambled eggs for dinner sometimes, but I'd worked hard today, and felt the need of more substantial, not to mention yummier sustenance.

After a short search, I found my car keys buried under a pile of early renewal offerings for the one magazine to which I subscribe and for which I had completely lost track of my actual renewal date. I grabbed the keys, tossed the renewals into recycling, and stopped.

If I went out for dinner, I'd likely be coming home to a dark and empty house, an unnerving prospect. And after last night, how could I be sure the power would be on when I returned? I still had no idea why it had gone out last night. The batteries in the penlight I found in the kitchen junk drawer were dead. Rummaging through the house, I located two more flashlights, one a wind-up model and one with weak batteries. The big problem with wind-up flashlights is that you have to be willing to stand a few moments in the dark cranking the otherwise useless thing before you can expect to get any light out of it.

On the other hand, at least with a wind-up, you will eventually get real light. A battery-operated flashlight with dead batteries is about as useful as a rock, although, I thought as I hoisted its weight in my hands, it might make a useful weapon. I chose the wind-up model and took it with me to the car. I could crank it until it was charged before emerging from the safety of my locked car, should I need its assistance. For extra insurance, I made the rounds, turning on lights so that, at least if the power was on when I returned, the house would be ablaze with light.

At the last minute I changed my mind about the dogs and put them back in the house. They wouldn't want to be stuck in the car while I went to dinner, and with them there to greet me I wouldn't have to walk into an empty house later this evening.

A dark sedan with a red, white, and blue decal, logo of the United States Postal Service on the door was indeed parked in front of the roadhouse. Illegally, I might add. It was flanked by the newest and shiniest county sheriff's SUV in the department, also parked illegally. Funny how installing those sidewalks and curbs seemed only to encourage illegal parking in that popular spot. Amanita must be beside herself with fury at her failure to enforce those rules. Even Bryce's truck was backed along the side of the roadhouse.

That new SUV must belong to, as Bryce had said, the real sheriff, not a lowly deputy. My friend Detective Muñoz was nowhere in sight, although that was not a big surprise. Muñoz likes to focus on more serious crimes like homicides, and in any case, as Bryce had said, the postal service probably has its own detectives to investigate postal crimes.

Sheriff Dugan stood at the edge of the porch, his uniformed belly protruding over his belt. He gazed at what he could see of

Arroyo Loco. I recognized him immediately from the numerous campaign posters, billboards, and brochures that had flooded the county during the last election. In person, the shock of curly chestnut hair falling over his wrinkled forehead looked even more fake than it had on the posters. His was the kind of toupee that begs to be stared at, and was perched on his bald head at a peculiar angle. Possibly he'd knocked it loose when he removed his hat.

Standing behind me, Freda whispered, "Ooh, so handsome." I tried to turn in time to see her face, but couldn't really tell if she was being facetious.

Behind her, Helen said, slightly louder than was strictly necessary, "Freda, you think every man in a uniform is handsome." Freda jabbed her elbow backwards, catching Helen on the sharp edge of her hip bone. I turned away and tried to pretend I had not seen either one of them.

Sheriff Dugan was still watching and had by then zeroed in on Graciela, standing across the road. She wore her shoulder holster again, and held her gun in one hand. She was explaining something about the gun to Jessica, who leaned close. The two of them shifted their gaze to a magazine Graciela held in her other hand. Didn't look like the usual fashion catalog.

"I don't recall issuing a permit for that woman to open carry in this county," the sheriff said. "Any of you know why she's waving than gun around?"

Christopher was the only one to jump to Graciela's defense. "She's scared, Sheriff. We're all kind of nervous with what's been happening. We've got families to protect." He paused. "Or at least some of us do."

Was that some kind of a dig at those of us who weren't raising children? As though we wouldn't be as concerned for everyone's safety?

"I get that," the sheriff said. "I know you're all nervous. But, ya know, when you're scared, that's the worst time you should be carrying a weapon. When your emotions are high, that's when you're gonna shoot the first thing that moves."

I kept my mouth shut, but Bryce cut me a look. They all knew those were my sentiments exactly. Maybe the words would have more impact coming from the sheriff.

Sheriff Dugan wasn't through. "She'd better put that thing away and lock it up good, or I'm gonna have to haul her off to the county hoosegow. Maximum sentence is three hundred and sixty-four days for violation of California gun laws." He turned to Christopher. "You want to go deliver that message, son? If I have to do it, I'll have to write her up, make it official."

"Uh, okay." Christopher did not look excited about being the bearer of what Graciela would consider bad news.

"And tell her I'd better not hear any more reports about her carrying that gun." He slid his gaze to each of us standing there on the porch. I don't know about anyone else, but I had the strangest feeling I had just been soundly scolded.

As I watched, a tall gaunt man I took to be the postal inspector finished sticking wide tape across the surface of all twenty or so mailboxes mounted on the front wall of the roadhouse. My box is located on the second row down, about eight from the left, nowhere near the three where tampering had occurred, but even so, it now sported a wide stripe of yellow tape across the front. I already had my key out, all set to retrieve today's delivery, although I wasn't expecting anything of more consequence than the usual handful of Bed Bath & Beyond coupons and Papa Murphy's fliers.

"Hey, what's the deal here?" I said, forgetting I was addressing a big-shot postal inspector and the real sheriff. "Nobody messed with my box. Why is there tape all over my box?"

"Sorry, ma'am," the postal inspector said. The nameplate pinned to his tweed blazer read "T. Pickard," and under that, "USPS Postal Inspector."

He continued, "All these boxes must be sealed and the mail impounded while we investigate the tampering." I tipped my head back and looked at him in dismay.

"Yeah, Estela," Bryce piped up. "This is a federal crime, you know?" Somebody should slap that boy, I thought. My back hurt from all that digging I'd been doing, and I was really beginning to feel the ill effects of lying awake half the night, the power off for unknown reasons, and unseen things bumping against the house. Not to mention, dinner time was approaching and I was increasingly hungry.

Postal Inspector T. Pickard wasn't done with the bad news. "And I'm afraid we're going to have to suspend mail delivery to this location until these boxes can be repaired. You'll all have to go to the main post office in town to collect your mail until repairs or a replacement can be made."

This pronouncement was greeted with angry groans. "Can't one of us pick up the mail for everyone here?" Christopher asked, not unreasonably.

"No, I'm afraid not," Postal Inspector Pickard said. "Each of you will have to present identification before the clerk can give you your mail."

"What a headache!" I said, and I believe I spoke for all, especially those who were occupied at work during normal business hours, and older folks who did not usually drive much if at all. Helen plopped onto the steps, uncharacteristically putting her head in her hands. Apparently this bit of bad news was hitting her especially hard. I sat beside her.

"Got you down, huh?" I said, patting her shoulder.

"All at once," she said. "It all happens at once." We shared a few seconds of companionable silence, me patting, she with her head hanging. "You know, Grant is working double-shifts. They still can't find that damned escapee. They've even got the FBI on it because he might have gone over state lines by now. And so I either have to get out of bed at oh-dark-thirty and drive him to work, and then stay up until the middle of the night to bring him home, or go without a car all day. Now this guy tells me I have to drive to town to get my mail. It's just too much."

I kept patting. I'd never seen Helen melt-down before. What could I do? "I know, I know. It's just the last straw, isn't it? Say, Helen, would you like to go into town with me for dinner? I'm on my way out now."

From somewhere above us, Freda overheard. "Ooh, yes! That would be fun. I would love to go to dinner."

"Can we go to that new brew pub place?" Helen said. "I hear the pub menu is really great."

"Oh, don't we want to go someplace nicer than that?" Nina said. "Someplace with tablecloths at least."

And we were off, another cat-herding adventure, four of us. I had to fold the backseat into the position to accommodate humans and brush off some dog fur, but we had a great time, Nina coped with a brew pub menu, and we laughed so hard, by the time I got home I had forgotten all about being frightened. I slept hard almost all night, awakening only long enough to visit the bathroom at four thirty-eight, right after the gunfire.

Shiner shook his collar at seven Sunday morning, his signal that he was fed up with sleeping and ready to go to his backyard to continue his nap in a conveniently placed ray of rising sun. I'd already peeled one eye open before I remembered the gunfire. Or was that a dream? No, I distinctly remembered hearing the sharp sound, three or four shots, and I recalled seeing Shiner in the bathtub when I visited the facilities. The tub is his go-to place when he's startled by any loud sounds.

My phone had not rung, nor had my mobile ding-a-linged an incoming text, so apparently neither the event triggering the gunfire, nor the aftermath had been of any consequence. Or else Bryce was finally catching on that he did not need to recruit my attention to everything that happened in Arroyo Loco.

The methodical raking around my new plantings had revealed the comings and goings of a variety of critters overnight. Most of the tracks were avian in nature, with three tiny toes pointed forward and one backward. Approaching from the canyon side, a set of small mammal paw prints, claws retracted, circled the bird bath and tracked to the edge of the newly planted area, disappearing into the fallen leaves and forest detritus there.

Retracted claws usually means cat tracks, and these were too small to be a bobcat. I was betting Helen's escaped cat Mocha had paid me a visit last night. I'd have to share the happy news that he was evidently safely surviving in the wild. The only other track of interest was something slithery in the soft dust near the sidewalk. I took comfort in the fact those slithery marks were far from the house. In spite of the fact that they loved freshly turned soil to root in, no boar tracks marred my rake marks, the bird bath remained upright and half-full, and all of my new plants were still in the ground.

I decided to fix a nice breakfast and then take Shiner and Scout to the beach for a good long run. I'd already put in a couple of long days digging holes and I deserved a break. I could pick up another bag of worm-castings at the garden store, and maybe I'd even treat myself to a store-bought coffee and a pastry for the beach a bit later. All the pastry I'd been eating lately, it was no wonder my cholesterol was disturbingly high.

Alas, no pastry was in my immediate future. A clot of my neighbors stood in the road in front of Graciela's house, and a sheriff's department SUV, one of the more battered and older-model ones, was just pulling out onto the highway.

When the group caught sight of my Subaru headed their direction, several folks stepped farther into the road, waving their arms and blocking my path, as though they thought I might try to cruise blithely past, which I was sorely tempted to do. Unwilling to actually mow anyone over, I pulled to the side and climbed out to join them and find out what all the excitement was about, leaving both dogs waiting for me in the car.

In fits and starts, the story emerged from multiple sources about the gunfire earlier this morning. As I had witnessed myself, it ceased after three or possibly four shots. The testimony varied as to exactly how many shots. In fact, several people had slept blissfully through the whole event and did not hear even one shot. Like myself, others had heard the sounds, but thought they were likely of no consequence and had gone back to sleep. We even got a couple of the "I thought it was just a car backfiring," excuses. In any case, no one had called anyone else at four thirty-eight in the morning. It was only now, in the full light of day, that the stories were being shared.

As it turned out, at least a couple of folks had spent all night sitting in darkened windows, watching. Their idea of a neighborhood patrol. They reported having seen people, or a person, wandering along our canyon road before dawn that morning, although the descriptions of what had been seen varied.

Raymond shared that at some time after the gunfire, he had clearly seen a large wolf trotting past his house toward the highway. He insisted it had been much too large to have been a coyote. We are all quite familiar with coyotes in this coastal mountain canyon, and unlikely to mistake them for anything else. No other witnesses came forward to corroborate his sighting, so Raymond's account of the wolf had to stand on its own.

Two others gave reports of humans darting from shadow to shadow. One witness said he had seen a small person and the other described what she observed as "a giant." Most folks, especially those who had been sound asleep and not seen anything, agreed the wanderer must have been the prison escapee. Their reasoning was that the rest of us law-abiding folks have already had the bejesus scared out of us, so none of us are going to be skulking around outside after dark.

Freda insisted she had distinctly heard a woman's voice crying in the night, which freaked several of us out. A wailing sound, she said, like a woman haunted by sadness. After further questioning, Freda admitted she had heard this from her bed after being awakened by the shots, and didn't bother to arise to check into the source. I contributed the fact that many people experience dream states so vivid they are hard to distinguish from reality, and maybe that explained Freda's experience. Mostly, folks seemed to dismiss Freda's tale as a faintly remembered dream. Mostly.

CHAPTER THIRTEEN

Of course Graciela was the likeliest suspect in the firing of a gun in Arroyo Loco. Again grim-faced, she had just been slamming inside when I'd pulled up and the deputy sheriff drove away. Helen admitted to calling law enforcement about an hour previous, after confirming with Raymond that shots had actually been fired. Prior to that, she suspected the whole thing might have been a figment of her sleep-deprived imagination.

Since the gunshots were long past and Graciela insisted she had nothing to do with them, the deputy sheriff who had responded to Helen's call made quick work of his investigation and left without placing blame on anyone. Really, the only consequence of his visit had been to infuriate Graciela. It did sound as though Arroyo Loco had been a lively place through this past night and into the morning, but I was not one bit sorry that I had missed it all.

Since even those who claimed to have watched a stranger creep through our neighborhood had declined to investigate further, our conclusions had to be based on general opinion. After much discussion, the conclusion was reached that the person that had been seen must have been the dangerous escaped prisoner, in spite of the varied descriptions.

By that time, the group had grown to include pretty much everyone coming and/or going through Arroyo Loco and, between my car pulled over to the side of road and the crowd gathered in the middle, the road was impassable. Bryce's battered red mini-pickup cruised up and stopped. Bryce's hair was slicked to his skull and he was attired in a shiny black suit jacket and white dress shirt, with a patterned necktie snugged tight enough to constrict his air flow. His mother, Alice, must have dressed him. She sat in the passenger seat wearing a dress suit in navy blue. A matching Pat Nixon pill box hat squashed her fluffy gray 'fro, and her face was heavily made up. Sunday morning, and it was no big mystery where they were headed.

"Yes, yes," Alice said, "and after the service, Bryce is taking me to lunch. And to bingo after that!" Alice was clearly very excited about the day ahead. Apparently, her happiness was not shared by her son. Bryce's expression could only be described as glum.

"You people need to move out of the road, Estela. We're already late."

Folks shuffled closer to Nina's house, allowing Bryce to go on his way. About that time, Lauren's new girlfriend's lime-green Kia rolled along side and stopped. Lauren and Kelly joined our group in the middle of the road.

"We're leaving," Lauren said. "After the break-in we're both scared, and Kelly can't take it any more. We're going back to her house in town until things chill here." I nodded in understanding, while at the same time wondering what would become of those of us who stayed behind if enough of our neighbors left. My nearest relative was a cousin near Santa Barbara who lived in a house too small to accommodate the dogs and me, and far enough away to make the commute annoyingly long.

"Did you hear the woman last night?" Freda asked her next door neighbor. "The one who was wailing and crying?" She turned to Kelly. "Did you hear her, honey? After those gunshots?" Kelly watched Freda as she talked, but shook her head slowly.

Lauren reached into the visual field of both and used her fingers to make moving signs. At the same time she said, "Kelly is deaf, Freda. She didn't hear anything."

"Oh, I am so sorry," Freda said, flustered. "How could we not know before this? I am so sorry, dear." She gave Kelly an earnestly sad look and patted her arm.

"I didn't hear anyone crying," Lauren said. "No, the reason we're leaving is because our clothes were taken off the clothesline last night, and some of them were stolen. Between that and being broken into that night while we were gone, we've had it."

While the rest of us made noises of shock and dismay, Christopher whipped out a ball point pen and wrote on the back of a tattered envelope also extracted from his back pocket. "I'll add this to the list of mischief and mayhem," he said. "Can you tell me exactly what happened, Lauren?" He stood, his pen poised for whatever additional information he could fit on the remains of the envelope.

"I'm a bit embarrassed to say, I forgot to bring the clothes in until well after dark," she said. "I decided I would get them in the morning, you know. But this morning all of the clothes were neatly folded on my back steps. Well, except for a couple of stray socks that had been dropped in the dirt. And when I brought the pile of clothes inside, we saw that one bath towel and a flannel shirt were missing. I checked everywhere, but couldn't find those things. Except for the socks I found in the dirt. Someone took the bath towel and the shirt and put the rest of the clothes on the porch. It's all too creepy for us. We're not going to stick around to see what happens next."

"Oh dear," Freda said. "I will feel quite lonesome up there with you girls not right next door to watch over me. Do you think, perhaps I should leave also? But where would I go?"

Jessica's packing us right now," Christopher said. "Those gunshots were the end of it for us. The rest of you can stay here, but I have a family. I have to take care of my family. We're leaving." He gave a disgusted shake of his head, but never said aloud the "to hell with the rest of you" that was written all over his face.

I wanted to mutter something about "rats leaving a sinking ship." On the other hand, I knew I would probably be packing for a few days away myself if it wasn't for the fact that Diego and Alex would be returning tomorrow. I would feel much safer with them home again with me. Only one more night to get through.

Lauren and Kelly squeezed back into the Kia. Clothes were piled on the backseat, and suitcases jammed underneath those. Kelly edged her car to the side of mine and they pulled onto the highway. We waved a sad goodbye.

Not five minutes later, Helen's phone dinged with an incoming text. "Something from Lauren," Helen said as she opened it.

Loose dog on highway. What to do?

"Sounds like your bailiwick, 'Stel'," she said, handing me the phone. "What else does she say?" Helen loomed over me, trying unsuccessfully to read the tiny screen.

"She says," I said, typing clumsily with both thumbs, "they found a dog loose on the highway. I'm telling her to bring it back here." We waited another couple of minutes and the phone dinged again. I read her response out loud.

"She says, 'Bring it back how exactly?'."

"Yeah, how exactly 'Stel? Isn't capturing loose dogs up your alley? How do you grab a loose one?"

"Well, for goodness sake," I said, typing again.

Put a leash on, put in car

I shook my head, and grumbled to Helen, "This is not rocket science. It's a dog." Another ding-a-ling sounded.

Leash? No leash

This time using a single forefinger I typed my reply.

Open car door dog will get in

And Lauren's reply,

Worked. Now where do I ride?

"Wow," Helen said. "That must be one big dog if he took up the whole passenger seat."

And we saw that it was indeed a large dog when, not three minutes later, the Kia returned in front of Nina's porch. The alert pointed ears and large head of a German shepherd poked through the sun-roof. The dog's body filled the passenger side. It appeared that Lauren had slid herself in sideways across the loaded backseat. Kelly and Lauren crawled out, but the dog stayed put.

"Wow," Helen said again, in awe. "Look at the size of those teeth." Stressed, the dog panted, revealing a whole mouth of shiny white sharp teeth with canines at least an inch long.

Kelly signed urgently as Lauren watched. "Yes," Lauren said to the rest of us, "Now how do we get him out of there? Look, there's something white on his shoulder. He's going to smear that on the upholstery."

Helen agreed. "Yeah, and what do we do with him once we do get him out? The last thing we need is another complication."

"Do we have to take him to animal control?" Freda asked. Her voice was shaky, but she at least sounded more compassionate. "Won't they kill him? We could use him as a guard dog, couldn't we? We could sure use a guard dog around here."

"Why would you haul a strange dog all the way into town to animal control?" Christopher had taken several steps back. He looked as though he was ready to sprint away at the least sign of any threat to his personal safety. "Don't they come out and get strays? You know, with that loop thing on their neck? He looks dangerous."

Raymond gazed at the dog still sitting, tall and confident in the vinyl seat. "You know," he said slowly, "I think that might just be the wolf I saw in the dark last night."

"A wolf!" Freda's voice hit a high squeaky pitch.

"Oh, geez!" Christopher echoed in a lower octave. "I'm getting Graciela. If it's a wolf, we should shoot it!"

I was thankful that it was Raymond's voice that bellowed, "No!" the loudest, although several others of us joined in the chorus.

I followed Raymond's comment with, "For pity's sake Christopher, where's your head?"

Raymond glared at the younger man. "My point was, I thought it was a wolf last night, but now I see he's a German shepherd, someone's pet dog."

"Yes," I said, "where's your heart, too, Christopher? This is someone's beloved friend! Besides which," I added, "even if this was a wolf, shooting it would be illegal and stupid. And anyway, it's not a wolf. The last wild wolf roaming California was shot and killed in the nineteen twenties." Christopher kept moving away, but veered more in the direction of his own porch than toward Graciela's.

"So ... " Lauren said in a tentative tone, "What do we do now? Kelly and I need our car back."

Kelly crooned at the shepherd, patted her leg, and in general, encouraged the dog to exit the vehicle. The dog was beginning to look sleepy, knees starting to buckle, chin resting on the roof of the car.

"How are we going to get him out of there?" Lauren said.

"For starters," I said, "as is perfectly obvious, this dog is a female."

"She's a girl?" Freda said, suddenly more friendly toward the dog.

"Yes," I said, "and she's got a collar on. I'll bet there's some identification under that fur." Slowly, I stepped onto what used to be called the running board so I could reach the dog's head. I stretched the back of my hand toward the open mouth and sharp teeth. The dog sniffed, then licked my hand. An audible sigh marked the collective release of breath as my friends saw the dog wasn't going to chomp on my hand. I stroked the side of the dog's snout and gentled my voice. "Hey, girl, you're lost aren't you? Probably scared, too." I rummaged in the fur near the fabric collar until I felt a small metal tag. Pulled that gently toward me. "Helen, can you read this? I don't have my reading glasses. And somebody write this down."

Nina disappeared inside while Helen read out loud. "Luna."

"So her name is Luna," I said. "Hi, Luna. What are you doing wandering out on the highway by yourself? We need to find your people." By that time, Nina was back with paper and a pen.

"Nina, can you take down this phone number?" I elbowed Helen and she read off the number on the tag.

"It also says 'reward'," she added, still reading. "I wonder how much?"

"I'll go call right now," Nina said as she turned and hurried up her steps. She was back in a flash. "Guess what! Luna lives in the very next canyon, right over there across the arroyo behind Christopher's place! They were thrilled to hear we have her! She said they'd be right over."

Nina had hardly finished talking before a well-broken-in pickup truck took the turn off the highway with a squeal and stopped in front of our gathering. A short round older woman dressed in worn jeans and a plaid shirt bounced down from the driver's side. At the same time, the shepherd pulled her head through the sun roof, squirmed out of the Kia, and bounded toward the woman. A joyful reunion ensued in which there could be no doubt that the shepherd and the woman belonged to each other.

After a series of hugs, exclamations, and excited yelps, the woman dropped the tailgate on the pickup and the shepherd jumped into the bed. The woman came forward to introduce herself.

"Marie Keller," she said, stretching out her hand to Helen who was nearest. "Most people call me Mama."

That was awkward. I'd already had enough Mamas in my life, beginning of course with my own dear sainted and long-suffering (on my account, I'm afraid) mother. There was a brief time when, during a very short and ill-fated marriage, my erstwhile husband's mother insisted I call her Mama. That lasted less time than our wedded bliss.

"Or Mama Keller," the woman said, moving on to vigorously shake Raymond's hand. "I b'lieve we've met, Mr. Watts?" Raymond looked confused, but since Mama Keller had his name correct, she must have been right about the two of them having met before. She made her way from person to person in our small group, nodding, smiling and shaking hands. Her hands were plump and warm, I noted, when she made it to me, and her eyes were wreathed in crinkly smiling wrinkles.

"We live just over there, across the arroyo." She waved off to her right. "You know, behind Tee's little house. In fact, Tee and I were good friends. That was a lovely service wasn't it? We really miss Tee. My son Gerald was friends with Thomas, too, all the time he was growing up. I guess Thomas and Margaret are gone, too. Moved into town, did they? Well, just as well to be closer to the market and what all ... " Mama Keller did not show any signs of slowing until Helen interrupted her.

"So how long have you lived there? Considering how close you are, it's kind of surprising we haven't met you and Gerald before." Helen sounded the tiniest bit suspicious.

"Oh, gracious, I don't even remember how long it's been. Since Gerald was diagnosed anyway. We should have come over sooner, you know, to say hello, but the way we live ... we're awake most of the night, sleep all day. The time just never seemed right. Anyway, I can't thank you enough for finding Luna and getting her safely back to us. She's Gerald's dog. He's been so upset since last night when she ran away. He won't even come out of his room."

I glanced at Mama Keller's passenger seat for a glimpse of this Gerald, but there was no one there. Guess the boy was genuinely so upset he wouldn't even come out of his room to retrieve his beloved dog.

"Oh, Gerald's not with me," Mama said making eye contact with me. "He's waiting at home." I nodded slowly. "In fact," she said, gazing slowly at each of us, "Gerald said someone fired a gun at them early this morning?" Nina and Raymond nodded solemnly, and Mama Keller went on. "Gerald said the gunfire scared Luna and she took off running. We've both been so afraid she might have been ... injured, or that she would get hurt on the highway. She looks okay though, don't you Luna?" Mama stuck her hand into the bed of the truck and ruffled the soft cream fur on Luna's chest. "Luna is Gerald's Canine Companion for Independence dog. She's quite valuable, and precious to us. She's Gerald's lifeline to the outside world."

The more Mama Keller talked, the more confused I felt. Apparently, I wasn't alone.

Freda peered over at the dog, whose tongue lolled long and pink. "What is a canine for independence dog?" she asked. "Is your son Gerald blind?"

"Well, sort of," Mama said. "He's not blind at all, but he has special needs. He's photosensitive. His skin burns and develops cancers if he is exposed to any sunlight at all. He has to stay indoors during the daylight hours. He can only go outside at night, and even then he has to wear long pants, sleeves, a hat. He wanders at night, and hikes all over these hills. It's really the only fun he has. And so Luna travels with him every night. We think she helps him see better in the dark, and avoid danger. Did you know there are wild boar in these hills? Those guys can be terrifying if they surprise you.

"And Luna helps Gerald find his way home, too, sometimes. She's already nine years old, but she still goes everywhere with Gerald. You know, when he wanders at night. No one has ever shot at them before, though."

"Your son only goes out at night?" Nina said. "He can never be outside in the day?"

"It's an allergy to the ultra-violet rays in sunlight," Mama said. "In non-effected people, exposure to sunlight might cause skin damage and cancer after sixty years. For those allergic to sunlight, like Gerald, the same damage will occur after only three years of exposure. And it took us until Gerald was about three years old to figure out he has this allergy, so we have to be really careful now. He does sometimes go out in the day time, but he has to protect his skin from exposure to the sunlight, so he wears long sleeves, you know?" She demonstrated by stroking both of her own arms. "And long pants and knee socks, and a big hat with a wide brim. Or else he likes to wear the red curly wig thing that pulls over his head like an old-fashioned bathing cap. That's when he dresses like a clown. That clown outfit is a great way to cover up from the sunlight, and have some fun at the same time, you know, going to birthday parties and the like. He also has to smear on this white make-up, Mehron it's called, all over his face. Big gloves, sunglasses. He even learned to make animals out of balloons to round out his clown character. You should see him, he's so cute. So, anyway … "

CHAPTER FOURTEEN

If my memory served, we had indeed met Gerald, the clown, a couple of years back at little Shawn's birthday party. He arrived and then disappeared without so much as a word, leaving behind a collection of colorful and oddly tied balloons as the only testament to his presence. I've always wondered where that clown came from. It must have been Gerald, on one of his rare daylight outings. Thinking about my encounter with that rather tall clown raised another question for me.

"Not to be too personal, Mama Keller, but how old is your son, Gerald?"

"Ah, well, uh, we recently celebrated Gerald's thirtieth birthday. He can't live on his own, you see, because of his condition. And he doesn't really have any friends, you know, since Thomas and his mother moved away. So he lives with me and I take care of him. You see?"

I nodded. A thirty year-old clown. That was a little creepy. Then again, I could understand Gerald's desire to be out in the world now and then. At least that was one mystery solved.

Maybe more than one, if some of the mischief we'd experienced could be explained by Gerald's antics.

Helen's brow was deeply furrowed. "No offense, ma'am, but I think someone here in Arroyo Loco would have noticed a clown roaming in this neighborhood at night."

"And complained about it," Nina added. There was a general nodding of agreement to this pronouncement.

"Oh, no," Mama said. "Gerald only goes out in his clown outfit during the day. You wouldn't see him at night in that get-up. At night when he and Luna go out he just wears regular clothes."

Freda had lowered a scowl at Mama Keller and followed her chatter with a nodding head, much in the way school girls nod along with a swinging rope, waiting for their turn to jump in. Finally Mama paused for a breath, giving Freda the opening she had been waiting for.

"And tell me, Mrs. Keller ... "

"Call me Mama, please. Only my lawyer calls me Mrs."

"Yes, well, in any case, tell me," Freda said, "does Gerald like tomatoes?"

"Oh, uh-oh," she hemmed and hawed, sighed and then shrugged. "Yes, the other night he did bring home a handful of those cherry tomatoes. He knows I love them. I did ask him where he got them, and he said he found them. Were they yours? I've given him a good talking-to about taking things that aren't his, but he still sometimes comes home with something. He's heard that lecture before. It goes in one ear and out the other. At night, you see, when he finds things, there's usually no one else there, so it's very tempting for him to bring things home. I've finally got him to leave things, you know, like tools?

He mostly leaves those things where he finds them, but food, you know, like fruit on a tree? He does still bring that sort of thing home sometimes. Were they yours? I have to admit, they were so delicious ... "

"Purely out of curiosity, Mrs. Keller," I said, "has Gerald ever brought home something like a lawn chair, or a bicycle?"

"Oh, dear." She put her hand over her mouth for a moment. "Not for years, but yes, I am afraid that is the sort of thing I had to talk to him about. Has someone lost their bicycle lately? Because he's not brought one of those home in years."

Because the missing bicycle had long since been replaced, I decided not to be specific. "No, no, not for years." I reassured her. "I was just curious."

Lauren had been frantically signing to Kelly throughout this conversation, trying to relay the information to her deaf friend. Kelly stopped her and signed something back. Lauren turned to Mama Keller, interrupting her. "Did Gerald come home last night with a couple of new ... " Kelly jabbed Lauren's arm and signed again. "Yes," Lauren said, "did he come home with a new and expensive flannel shirt?"

"No, no," Mama Keller shook her head. "My Gerald would not steal clothing. He's really a very good boy. If he found your shirt, he would put it on your porch. He'd probably fold it, too. I've explained to him many times about not bringing home things that are not his. I know sometimes he does things he shouldn't do, but that's mostly because he spends so much time alone. You know, without immediate supervision. He did bring me those tomatoes, but he's a good boy. He wouldn't steal your clothing."

I considered this information. "So what I'm hearing is that, while someone did steal Lauren's shirt ... "

Kelly poked Lauren again and Lauren said, "And a big bath towel."

"... Yes, a shirt and a big bath towel. Someone stole those, but it wasn't Gerald. Gerald may have folded the remaining clothes and left them on your porch, but if that shirt is gone, someone else took it."

"And the towel," Lauren added.

"Yes, whatever. In any case, we're talking about someone other than Gerald being the thief."

It was Helen's turn to poke me. Casting a quick wary glance at Mama Keller, Helen stage-whispered, "What is that thing you're always telling us, 'Stel'? The most likely answer is the most likely to be true? We've already placed Gerald at the scene of the tomato theft a few nights ago. Isn't it most likely that he also took the shirt? I mean, either he took it, or you have to make the assumption there's more than one guy wandering out here at night taking stuff."

That, of course, had been exactly my point, but I could see it would bear repeating. Helen had Ockham's philosophy slightly garbled, although she was heading in the right direction with it.

"Yes," I said. "Well, not so much the most likely answer as the one requiring the fewest assumptions. But now we have some additional evidence. 'Mama' says Gerald did not take those things, so it sounds as though we have more than one night-time wanderer. On the other hand, does it really make any sense that the same guy would both steal the shirt and also fold the remainder of the laundry and leave it on the porch? If someone wanted the shirt, wouldn't he just grab it and go?"

"And a big bath towel," Lauren added.

Mama Keller had developed a deep scowl and a nervous tic in one eye. "I don't know what you folks have got going on here, but if there is a thief wandering about, I'm not letting Gerald come over here again. Actually, he's not coming back anyway, what with some gun nut shooting at innocent boys and their dogs. Luna and I are going home."

With that, she climbed into her truck, back and filled, and headed onto the highway. We stood and watched in silence.

Helen, hands on her hips, said, "Wow, what a motor mouth. Even I couldn't compete with her."

"Yes," I agreed. "Well, that was awkward, but she has a point. Do we know who was doing the shooting?"

Nina was stuck on a previous issue. "I've never met Gerald, but it doesn't seem ... from talking to his mother, it doesn't seem likely that he would do things like try to pry open mailboxes or spray paint on Graciela's house. Maybe we really do have more than one nocturnal visitor here?"

Freda placed a hand over her mouth, and her eyes got wide, mirroring the fear that was sinking in for all of us at that possibility.

"And the second guy might be the guy who shot at Gerald," Christopher said.

"Yeah, right," someone said. It might have even been me. We all rolled our eyes. The Arroyo Loco Homeowners Association might have a guideline discouraging the rolling of eyes during formal meetings, but no one could stop the practice during informal discussions carried out on the sidewalk. We might not have any evidence who had fired a gun three or four times at four-thirty-eight this morning, but we all had the same suspicion.

"I have an idea," Helen said. She scuffed the toe of one shoe against the other in an apparent sudden shy attack. "I mean, I'm just trying to be helpful here ... "

"Yes?" I encouraged her with a rolling hand.

"Well, it's just that here we are trying to figure out who might be doing these things, and we're all watching and so on, and well, I have heard that when people lose one sense, their other senses become, well, more acute, and well ... I am just wondering if possibly ... Lauren's friend ... ?"

"Kelly?"

"Yes, Kelly. If Kelly here might possibly be able to see better than the rest of us and possibly she would be willing to go on watch for us?"

Impatience is rarely a successful approach to take with Helen, although I could barely contain myself.

"What do you mean, Helen? Do you mean you think Kelly might have enhanced night vision because she's deaf, or something like that?"

Helen gave me a defensive shrug. For my part, I carefully controlled any impulse to roll eyes or make a disgusted shake of my head.

"Anyway, Helen, Kelly is right here. Why don't you ask her yourself?" Belatedly, I noticed Lauren's fingers and hands dancing again, relaying the conversation to Kelly. Shaking their heads in silence, both young women climbed back in their small car and drove away from Arroyo Loco.

There being nothing else needing discussion at the moment, my dogs and I continued on our journey to the beach where we engaged in a long Sunday stroll for me, and a romp through the surf for them. We found, picked up, and hauled to the trash a half a garbage bag full of plastic straws, toothpaste tube caps, soggy plastic bags, a chunk of garden hose, and a host of other less-identifiable plastic objects. On this trip, we found nothing more sinister than that. As I stuffed the trash into the old oil drum put there for that purpose, I wondered if some of that plastic would eventually find its way onto a barge hauling garbage out to sea, and the same objects would wash ashore again. Who knew? In a couple of weeks, I could be picking the same objects up for a second time. Wonder why it's so hard for humans to understand the impact, both long and short term, of their own behavior on the rest of the world.

That was about enough self-reflection for me for the day. I stopped at Bon Temps for Creole red beans and rice, and a cardboard to-go container of sausage gumbo, making an exception to my no-meat policy. Maybe it's that the product itself, the sausage, is so far removed from its animal origins. Or maybe I like sausage enough that I'm not willing to sacrifice eating it to a moral principle. While enjoying the gumbo I've noticed that I do find myself trying not to think about the animal who unwillingly gave its life to feed me, so it's probably only a matter of time before I quit eating the sausage too.

For once, all was quiet in Arroyo Loco as I rolled past my neighbor's homes and parked in my own driveway. I reached for the door handle, then stopped. Something was off. It took a moment for me to realize that, not only was the screened porch door unlatched and swinging gently in the breeze, but the kitchen door also stood ajar. I sat and stared at it for a moment.

I will be the first to admit I sometimes do neglect to latch that porch door, and I have been known to leave the house without locking the kitchen door. Embarrassing, but true. However, I do not go away for hours and leave the doors standing open. The other half of the parking pad was empty, so Diego and Alex had not retuned early. Something was wrong.

Leaving the dogs safely in their back seat, I opened the car door and crept silently up the steps. Listened. Nothing. Went to stand in the kitchen doorway. Looked to my left, where the dining table stood empty, save for the tarnished copper napkin holder I had made in seventh grade shop, and few limp paper napkins. Looked to my right, into the kitchen area. The usual items stood in their usual places on the countertop, and nothing appeared to have been disturbed. But something wasn't right.

I scanned the whole open area before me. It wasn't what I saw, that caught my attention, but what I didn't see, as though there were holes in my visual field. Then objects began to come into focus. The five-foot wide console table where our flat screen had been sitting now held swirls of dust and a couple of loose wires. The shelf below that one gave me a blank stare, also strangely empty. The video cassette recorder we hadn't used in years was gone, as was the Sony Betamax on the shelf beside that one. Who would steal a Betamax, I wondered.

The drawers in the end tables had been left open, and their contents scattered on the floor nearby. The cabinet where I kept the too-easily-destroyed dog toys, or those that inspired flinging about with attendant likely breakage of decor stood open, the toys piled in front. The drawer next to my recliner had held mostly odd papers, used envelopes with cryptic notes scrawled on the back, the reminder to renew my Audubon membership that I was still trying to decide about, an address book. These were littered across the carpet.

What with the mess, it was hard to determine if any items besides the electronics were missing. Nevertheless, I had clearly been burgled. I hadn't moved from the doorway, so for all I knew, the culprit was still hiding inside. I backed away. From the comfort and safety of my driver's seat behind a locked car door, I dialed nine-one-one and reported the burglary. The dispatch officer wanted to know if the burglar was still inside, and I had to honestly answer that I didn't know. She said she'd send someone right away.

I sat there for a few minutes feeling mostly surprised. I think I was supposed to feel invaded or violated, but mostly I felt surprised. I knew it might take a good long while for the sheriff's deputies to arrive, although the possibility that the burglar might still be inside did seem to light a small fire under that dispatcher.

Deciding my wait might be less tedious and scary if I had company, I called Nina. She answered from somewhere in Pismo Beach where she was "visiting a friend," code for on a date. It was Sunday afternoon, so I shouldn't have been surprised. I just hoped she wasn't with that sketchy firefighter, Pete, again. Helen was home, and happy to come join in the excitement. While I waited for her arrival, I stared at the screened porch. My expensive new binoculars sat on the table there. Whoever had carried out the burglary had not been a very observant sort. Then again, I suppose it's not the brightest bulbs who go in for a life of crime.

The passenger door rattling startled me. When Helen leaned over and peered in through the sticky salt air and dog nose prints stuck on the window, I hit the unlock button. She climbed inside and joined me in staring at the open kitchen door. Shiner and Scout stood, and stretched their necks toward her for a friendly greeting. Helen rudely ignored them. The dogs threw themselves to the seat again, each making a loud and disgusted-sounding sigh as they settled.

"So you already called the cops?" she said.

I checked my phone for the time. "Yes, about twenty minutes ago. They're supposed to be on their way."

"And you don't know if the burglars are still inside?"

"No. I didn't hear anything, but I wasn't going to go looking for them."

We shared a long moment of silence.

"There's no back door on this place, right?" Helen asked.

"No. Well, this is the kitchen door right here." I pointed. "There's another door over here to the left. That's technically the front door, but it hasn't been used in years. There's a bookcase in front of it on the inside, and if someone tried to go out that way, that old porch would probably fall right off."

"Uh huh. My point was, if there is someone in there, this door here is the only way out, right? So we'd see them."

"Yes," I said. More silence. "I suppose they could climb out a window. You know, in the bedroom."

"You should put your dogs in the yard so they could bite anyone who tries to climb out the bedroom window."

I thought about her suggestion for a nanosecond. "Don't really want my dogs getting kicked by a burglar."

"They wouldn't bite him before he could do that?"

"Probably not. They might try to herd the guy. Don't think they'd bite."

"Humph." She craned over her shoulder to her right and started to ask if possibly Bryce or his parents had seen something from their house, then interrupted herself. "Oh, here comes a deputy, now."

CHAPTER FIFTEEN

An SUV decorated with the county sheriff's decal and the words "K9 Unit Stay Back" plastered on the sides pulled into the empty spot next to my car. Shiner and Scout stood again and gazed through the window at the new arrival. They looked for all the world as though they were reading the words on the side of the vehicle. The dark Belgian Malinois canine deputy was a faint outline inside the tinted windows. My dogs' tails began a slow wagging. They had either read the words painted on the vehicle, or were scenting the canine deputy. With border collies, you can never be sure which.

Helen and I climbed out and I went through the briefest of explanations for the deputy sheriff. He asked us both to get back inside the car, and got his partner out. Without so much as a woof, Shiner and Scout sat and watched as the two intimidating deputies climbed onto our porch. Holding to the dog's collar, the deputy knelt beside his canine partner in the open doorway.

Yelling so loudly we could clearly hear him from the safety of our car, the deputy said, "Anyone inside, county sheriff here!

Step into view now! Hands where I can see them!" He paused. "Step into view now, or I'm sending the dog in!" He paused again. "I'm sending the dog in on three!" The dog trembled with excitement and the muscles in his back haunches bunched, readying to leap after the burglar. "One ... two ... three!" And with that, the deputy released his hold on the dog.

I hated to see the dog race into what might be a deadly situation. The deputy had a gun, so I don't know why he didn't step inside himself instead of endangering the life of his dog. I understand the justification that threatening an attack by a dog would make some bad guys surrender, but if there was a bad guy in my house at that moment, he had not responded to the threats.

As it turned out, the dog did not get shot, principally because there was no one inside the house. And no one looked more disappointed at not finding a burglar than the dog, so maybe I'd misinterpreted her motivations. After disappearing inside for a minute or two, the deputy returned his partner to the backseat in his SUV and fed her a handful of treats. He stood and waved us out. I rolled all four windows about one-third of the way open, grabbed my Creole dinner, and Helen and I joined the deputy.

The three of us entered my house and walked slowly through every room. I popped my to-go bag into the refrigerator and followed the others. The bed in Diego's room had been rumpled, blankets pulled back, and pillows thrown on the floor. Drawers had been pulled out in my room and a few clothes scattered about. Thankfully, the drawer containing my "delicates" was undisturbed. The medicine cabinet in the bathroom stood open, but all appeared to be in place. I don't store anything in there of an illegal nature, or even any kind of controlled substance.

We settled into chairs at the dining table while the deputy, his name tag read M. Jackson, began filling out some paperwork. He asked about what I saw when I first arrived, and if there was any chance I could have left the house unlocked—there admittedly was—did anyone else have a key —too numerous to list—and anyway I hardly remembered who all had been given keys at one time or another. Helen claimed not to have one, which was a surprise to me. Deputy Jackson pointed out there was no evidence the door had been forced, leading to his conclusion that it had either been left unlocked or the burglar had had access to a key.

He pulled another form to the top of his clipboard. "Okay, then let's make a list of everything you know is missing. You'll probably notice additional missing items after I'm gone, but having a police report listing the items you notice missing now will help with your insurance claim. You might also want to call a locksmith and have this lock changed."

I turned a distressed expression to Helen. "I'll get on that," she said, pulling out her cell phone. "How about if I call that company Nina had over the other day?"

"Okay then, let's start with the living room," the deputy said, drawing my attention to the living area. "Your television went here, right?" He waved at the now-empty console, and I nodded. I think the shock was settling in, although I mostly felt excited, as though I was acting in a live television crime drama.

He waved again. "Looks to be about a 55 inch flat screen was here?" He was already writing that on the list before I could explain.

"No, not exactly," I said. "We were going to get a new one. The one that was there was old, and pretty small. Not the whole length of the console at all."

Deputy Jackson had already moved on. "Looks like some other components are gone, too. A sound system? A DVR?" He pointed at the empty shelves below where the television had stood.

"Uh, a Betamax was on that shelf," I said.

The deputy's pen stopped in mid-air poised over the next line on his list. His face was a blank stare. "A Beta ... what?"

"Max," came a familiar voice from the still-open doorway. "A Betamax. It was a brand of video cassette recorder and player. A real antique." My old friend Detective Muñoz stood there. Yes, I thought, this is exactly what this situation calls for, a professional detective. He nodded in my direction.

"Holy cow! The cavalry has arrived!" Helen said.

Muñoz's eyes slid across Helen without stopping. "What have we got here?" His question was directed at Deputy Jackson, but Helen answered.

"What we've got here is a brazen daylight burglary! Yet one more in a string of puzzling and malicious crimes. Nice to see you taking an interest," she added in a snide tone.

His eyes came back to her. "What's all the excitement about over at the roadhouse?"

"Now, you mean?" Helen asked. "I have no idea. I've been here with Estela for an hour." She turned to me. "Probably I should go, now that your detective friend is here." She stood. "The locksmith will be here first thing in the morning, Estela. I'd better go see what's going on ... " She mumbled a few more parting sounds, and was gone, leaving me to wonder how I was going to sleep knowing the burglar might have a key to my house.

From over the deputy's shoulder, Muñoz read the list of missing items. "Doesn't look like a whole lot," he said, and looked at me. "Did you check for valuables, jewelry, that kind of thing?"

"I don't have anything like that," I said, then stopped. "There is my mother's wedding ring ... but that's hidden. I don't think anyone could have found that. Still, I'd be really upset ... hang on, let me go look." Making sure they didn't follow me, I went to check my secret hiding place. Thank goodness, I found the ring right where I had hidden it. When I returned to the living room, Muñoz was standing in the kitchen doorway looking out.

"So, that house there is the only one that has a view of yours?" He pointed at Ernie and Alice Bantam's house, where Bryce lived in the converted garage below his parents.

"Yes, except if she's looking out her kitchen or bathroom window Freda can see at least my driveway and part of the porch. She might have seen something." Remembering our earlier encounter, I said, "Bryce and Alice left this morning and had plans to be gone almost all day, it sounded like. They probably didn't see anything. Maybe Ernie did, although he's in a wheelchair now, so he wouldn't have been able to stop anyone."

"He can use a telephone," Muñoz said, not making it clear whether he was asking a question or making a statement. He turned to the deputy standing behind him.

"Jackson, I want you to do a quick neighborhood check. Interview the Bantams. Whatever they may have seen or heard.

And anyone else you run into. Then check with Freda ... " he turned to me. "Freda ... ?"

"Von Leising," I supplied.

"Freda Von Leising. Anyone else who might have seen an unfamiliar car or truck coming or going. There's only this road to get in or out, right?"

"Yes." I confirmed.

"I'll keep an eye on the canine," Muñoz said as Deputy Jackson trotted out the driveway on his way to the Bantam's house. The two of us stepped back inside and Muñoz read over the list of missing items again.

"Not much here," he repeated.

"No," I had to agree.

"And what there is, well, I don't see much of value. Monetary value, anyway."

"That's true. Then again, a burglar could take pretty much everything I have and he still wouldn't get much of value. I'm not that into having all the latest stuff." I thought about those expensive new binoculars on the porch. I stuck my head out and checked. They still sat on the end table in clear view.

"What about Diego and Alex?" he said. "Anything of theirs missing? They must have computers, high-end devices?"

"Oh. Good question. I really don't know. Stuff in their room was scattered. I guess I'd better call them." I said this with dread, knowing Diego would be likely to blow a gasket, especially if it ultimately turned out I had left the door unlocked. Not to mention I would be disturbing their romantic weekend getaway. They were due home after work tomorrow, Monday, so calling now would interrupt their last evening away.

Muñoz stood watching the expressions flit across my face. Never one for lots of words, sometimes Muñoz knew exactly what I was thinking just by watching my face. Guess that's why they'd made him a detective.

He cleared his throat. "You know, the usual home burglary like this, they're looking for guns, jewelry, tools, drugs, anything small enough to easily carry and then sell. Things a shady pawn dealer would take. Nothing on this list looks like anything anyone would want to buy."

"What does that mean?"

He pushed his lips out while he thought. "Well, what it means to me is that you either had a young, naive burglar, you know, someone who didn't know what they were doing, or ... "

"Or what?"

He shook his head slowly. "Or this wasn't a real burglary."

"What do you mean by that?" I could hear my voice rising into a hysterical pitch. "You think I faked this? Why would I do that?"

"Calm down. I'm not saying you faked anything. I'm just asking, do you have any neighbors who might want to scare you, for example? Or someone who wanted to mess with you for some other reason? Someone who had reason to think you had something of value here, and tossed the place while looking for it?"

I shook my head no, but thought about his question. I couldn't think of anyone fitting that description. Yet here was the evidence. Someone had been here, rummaged through my house, and stole a few of my less-than valuable things. "Well, damn," I said, tears beginning to collect at the edge of my lids.

Muñoz draped his arm over my shoulder. "Come on, let's go sit on the porch and wait for Jackson to come back."

No sooner had we settled in than I remembered my dogs, still waiting patiently in the car. I let them out and brought them onto the porch so they could get out into their backyard. Scout went directly to the water dish and took a good long drink. Shiner stopped in the kitchen doorway, sniffing. He stretched his neck out and sniffed harder. There'd been at least three unfamiliar individuals inside there since Shiner had last entered, and he clearly was noticing the different scents. The deputy and his dog had left signs of their passing, as had the burglar.

Muñoz and I watched Shiner.

"Would he track the burglar?" Muñoz asked, still watching.

"I was wondering the same thing. You know, what would happen if I gave him the 'find' command. But there's already been too many other unfamiliar scents through there, I think. And anyway, Shiner has had a few scent work classes, but tracking is not his area of expertise ... yet. He's a herding dog. Almost any dog can do tracking, though, with the right training."

Loud stomping on the wooden steps and a squeal as the screened door opened alerted us to the return of the deputy.

"Couldn't locate anyone at the Von Leising house," he said. "Or anyone else in that part of the neighborhood. They must all be at the roadhouse, whatever that excitement is about." He glanced at us. "Even at my aunt's house." He shifted his gaze to me. "Delia Jackson. That's my aunt." I thought about interjecting something socially appropriate, like how nice it was to meet Delia's nephew and how proud she must be that he'd succeeded in landing a career with the sheriff's department, but decided that would be off-topic. I nodded and smiled instead.

Deputy Jackson consulted his notebook and continued his report. "Up here at this house that looks down on yours, Mrs. Alice Bantam said she and her son were out all day. They returned after Mrs. Nogales' car was already in the driveway here."

"Doctor," I said.

"Huh?"

"Just call me Estela," I said, shaking my head. I was getting punchy and tired.

"Uh huh. Okay. So Mrs. Bantam said she and her son did not see anything, and her husband ... uh, that's ... " He looked at his notebook again. "Ernie. Ernie Bantam told me he was napping and didn't see anything either."

"Napping all day?" Seemed unlikely to me, but Ernie's life had changed drastically since he'd had that accident a couple of years back and been confined to a wheelchair. What did I know?

"That's what he said. I didn't talk to the son. His mother said he's down at the highway with everyone else." Deputy Jackson snapped his notebook closed and changed his focus to Muñoz. "We could look into that?"

Muñoz tipped his head slightly to his left in a gesture that looked like "maybe," but at the same time he rose and moved toward the door. He had to pull his sedan forward before the deputy and his dog could be on their way.

Just as the canine unit pulled away, Grant and Raymond appeared together, walking up hill. They seemed an unlikely partnership, as I had not seen them together before. Raymond has a reputation as a confirmed consumer of national public radio, and Grant prefers sensationalist entertainment to actual news. Not only that, but Grant was carrying his shotgun over his shoulder, and you'd never expect to see Raymond anywhere near a gun of any kind.

That shotgun reminded me that Graciela is not the only person in Arroyo Loco who owned a gun. There probably were others, as well. Since Raymond was along, I had to assume they were not out to take pot shots at our few remaining wild boar or some other wildlife.

"Hey, fellas," I said. "Where you headed?" In my peripheral vision I saw Muñoz pull his vehicle back to the sidewalk, park, and get out. No surprise a member of the county sheriff's crew would be curious about guns being carried openly in Arroyo Loco.

One thing Raymond and Grant have in common is that they are sometimes annoyingly laconic. Not that I'm complaining. Heaven knows, we have plenty of neighbors here who are happy to fill any conversational space with meaningless banter, so a few who are prone to keep their mouths shut unless they have something useful to contribute are always appreciated. But at this moment, I was genuinely curious about their destination and intention.

Raymond finally waved generally in the uphill direction. This much I could have guessed. "Oh?" I said.

"Amanita's," he finally conceded.

"She left days ago. Friday, I think. She won't be home."

"Yeah," Raymond agreed, then sighed. "Thing is, a couple of the kids, Colleen and Sofia, they were out on those trails …

here." This time he waved at the hills surrounding our canyon, criss-crossed with deer paths and hidden alcoves. "They were out there last night, and they saw a light on at Amanita's."

Even though I could not see the house in question from my location, I gazed that way, squinting as I thought.

"Those girls shouldn't be out there on those trails at night," I said. "Anything could happen."

"The boys used to go out there all the time when they were that age," Raymond said, and I had to agree. Still.

"And as for a light," I said, "maybe Amanita left a light on to discourage burglars." I paused, caught Muñoz's gaze. "Apparently, we have a burglar in town."

Still looking uphill, Raymond added, "Said they saw someone moving inside. From on the trail. Said there was definitely someone in the house. We thought it wouldn't be a bad idea to go check."

Muñoz slapped the left side of his chest, checking for something. "Hang on. I'll go with you." He keyed the lock closed on his sedan and trotted to join Raymond and Grant. I thought about tagging along, but opted to nuke my dinner and feed myself and my hungry dogs instead. Be just my luck the burglar would return and really clean me out if I went off and left the house again, and I didn't want to take a chance on missing a meal.

There were still a couple of hours of daylight left by the time I finished my gumbo and french bread. Plenty of time to get the rest of those plants in the ground. I kept a look out for the guys returning from Amanita's. I hadn't heard any gunfire by the time Raymond and Grant came back by, but they had to step quickly onto the new sidewalk out front when a white

183

deputy sheriff's vehicle whizzed past, aimed in the direction from which the guys were returning. We all watched it disappear around the curve, and I turned to Grant, making a questioning gesture with my hands.

"Turns out, somebody did break in," Grant said.

CHAPTER SIXTEEN

"Someone broke into Amanita's?"

"Yup. Busted the lock on the back door. Looks like they ate or took pert' near ever bit of food in the kitchen there." Raymond was nodding right along with Grant's description.

"That's all they took was food?"

"Hard to say," Raymond said. "Have to ask Amanita. You know where she's gone to?"

All I could do was shake my head. Obviously no point in calling the phone number we all had for Amanita, her landline. Unless someone else was chummier with her than I knew about, we'd have to wait until she returned to tell her about the break in.

"Anyhoo," Grant said, "your pal Muñoz is gonna nail that back door shut, so's nobody can get in that way again."

"Food's all gone anyway," Raymond added. Grant hitched the shotgun higher on his shoulder and the two men continued their amble down hill.

Several minutes later, Muñoz appeared on the sidewalk. I rested against my shovel.

"They tell you what happened?" Muñoz asked.

"Yes. Grant said some food was taken. You think maybe Arroyo Loco should hire a crew of professional guards?"

Muñoz gazed silently away. Considering, I suppose, why anyone would hire professionals to guard cans of beans and boxes of crackers, or whatever had been in Amanita's kitchen. Then he said, "That's an idea," but his tone said he thought it was an entirely ridiculous one. We were all approaching our wits' end.

"I left the tech there to lift some prints, find some kind of evidence."

We let a short silence settle between us.

"This morning we found out who took Freda's tomatoes, and is responsible for some of the more innocent events we've experienced," I told him. "But there's still plenty left to explain. Whatever happened to that escaped prisoner?"

"Never found him. Assumption is, he caught a ride and is far away by now. We have a good description, and sooner or later someone will spot him. We'll get him."

"And in the meantime, someone is breaking in and stealing things all over Arroyo Loco. I suppose it's only a matter of time before someone gets hurt. What does the sheriff think we should do? What happens next?" My pitch approached a squeaky tone as I spoke, and my voice came out a lot more whiny than I intended.

Muñoz did not have any new ideas to add. "Get new locks," he said. As he left, he called over his shoulder, "We'll be in touch. Let us know if Diego finds anything of his missing."

Dreading the outcome, I punched Diego's number into my phone and listened to it ring. I was just starting to hope for voicemail when he answered. Using as few words as possible I explained the situation. After a brief consultation with his new wife, they decided to return here and search their own room for missing items. In a tired voice, he estimated they'd be back in three to four hours, which made it … I checked my phone for the time. They should be home sometime after midnight, a whole night early.

This being late summer, there was still enough light to see my new garden. I fixed a tall glass of iced tea and tracked down my current book, then curled on the porch swing to finish the day in peace. The light wasn't the best so I was unable to identify the tiny bird sipping at my new bird bath, and reading turned out to be impossible. The newly planted bushes were much too small to provide cover yet. Once those had filled out, they would give birds a place to hide and wait their turns at the bath, and I would really be able to get good looks at everyone visiting my yard.

I also wanted butterflies to drop by. Last spring I'd planted three Dutchman's pipevine plants on the lattice at the far end of the porch. They needed more water than nature here provides and had done well as long as I remembered to water them. I had seen several black swallowtail butterflies fluttering past this summer. As I sat in the silence of the gathering dusk, I could hear the caterpillars munching hungrily on the pipevine leaves. At least I hoped that was what I was hearing. Are termites big enough to make audible sounds while they devour an older wooden house?

That side of the porch and house face a gully filled with coyote brush and poison oak. The original pathway to the front entry runs along that side of the house. The porch and front door are still over there, although one now has to negotiate the pipevines and risk tumbling into the gully in order to get there. Since I've been here, I've always used the screened porch and kitchen door as my entry. I never use the old front door. As I sat there, I couldn't remember if I've ever locked that old door, or if the wooden steps leading to it were in any condition to use safely.

Deciding I would put all that on my to-do list, or at least on my list of home repairs to talk to Diego about, I took the dogs and myself off to bed. My last thought before drifting off was one of gratitude that Diego and Alex would be home soon, making tonight the last evening I'd be the only human here.

Once my head hit the pillow, I entertained myself by making a mental list of everyone to whom I had ever given a key to my house, for whatever seemed like a good reason at the time. Turned out to be a rather extensive list, but no one too sinister was on it. Thank goodness I fell asleep for a good couple of hours after that, because the rest of the night was not so restful. All three of us—the dogs and I—were startled awake at close to midnight by another of those loud bumps like the ones that had awakened me a couple of nights ago. This time I knew it was something bumping the house because the framed photograph of my parents hanging in the hallway rattled against the wall. Or maybe it was only a sonic boom from a rocket launched at Vandenburg Air Force Base. That happens sometimes.

I started to roll over, then stopped, thinking I heard creaking, like the sound an old nail makes when it's pulled from where it's lodged in wood, or a loose board on an old porch. I waited in my halfway turned over position, listening. I didn't have to wait long. The first creak was soon followed by a chorus of creaks, some scrapping sounds, and then a huge crash. It sounded like my whole house was falling apart.

Both dogs were on the bed with me in a flash. I'm never sure why I have such faith in those dogs to protect me from danger when it's obvious they are both big babies when it comes to scary stuff. Clearly they were expecting me to protect them.

I slipped on my bedroom scuffs and padded to the living room. There are no windows on the gully side of the house, so I couldn't see anything from there. The sounds of something, who knows what, sliding and thrashing echoed from the gully. I returned to the bedroom to pull on some pants and shoes. The dogs were still comfortably asleep on my bed, Scout having laid claim to my previously clean pillow. If I was going outside, I wasn't going alone. I made Shiner get off the bed and come with me, letting the older dog continue his nap.

We don't keep weapons of any kind in our house, so the most lethal thing I took with me was the windup flashlight. I tried to peer into the gully from the far end of the screened porch, but couldn't see much, what with the pipevine covering the lattice there. I did still hear the caterpillars munching. Did those guys never sleep?

Shiner and I crept down the steps and to that side of the house. The moon hadn't risen over the ridge yet, leaving the yard in darkness, and making whatever was going on in the gully invisible. I could see that wall of the house from where I stood at the corner of my new garden. And, with sort of a shock, but no huge surprise, I realized the old porch that used to lead to the front door was suddenly missing. The porch that had been hanging there for many years chose this night to pull loose and fall off. Presumably, whatever remained of it now lay below, hidden in the gully.

Or possibly the porch had not given way exclusively due to old age or termites. Anyone familiar with that porch would know enough to stay off of it. I think at one point I had even stretched some old yellow garden tie tape across the bottom step to warn neighbors to stay off, although that had probably long-since weathered away. In any case, it seemed likely that someone not blessed with common sense had chanced the climb, and possibly ridden the wreckage to the bottom of the gully. That porch was history.

As I came back past the new garden, moonlight broke over the ridge and threw the ground at the base of the bird bath into sharp relief. It wasn't until then that I noticed the tiny foot prints in the dust. Instead of the boar hoof prints I was expecting, or the tracks of a large domestic cat, or even the boot prints of some evil burglar or malicious vandal, what I saw were tiny sneaker prints circling the base of the bird bath. My little friend Eli, I suspected. What had that tyke been doing wandering out here at night?

Then I thought, what if Eli had been the one to climb on that porch and even now the small child lay gravely injured in the rubble below? What should I do? And what sort of a parent allows their child, hardly more than an infant, to go wandering off in the middle of the night? Or maybe Eli was a sleepwalker. Maybe his parents had no idea he'd been out here because the child was sleepwalking. A sleepwalker who evidently stops to put on his sneakers before heading out. Could happen, I suppose, but that seemed unlikely.

Should I call, or go over to the Rankin's, disturb the entire household, only to find out Eli was tucked safely in his bed? I had no way of knowing when those foot prints had been left. The truth was, I had been gone most of the previous afternoon. Trying not to disturb the track, I followed the small foot prints. They encircled the bird bath, and then trailed back out to the sidewalk. I could find no evidence the small sneaker-wearer had gone to the side of the house where the porch had fallen.

I sighed, unsure what to do. At least one issue was resolved. There was clearly no point in going back to bed, as sleep would surely elude me now. A flutter of soft feathers and movement brought my attention to the eave of the porch, where I was startled to see a large turkey vulture. The bird sat in silence gazing over my yard. The two of us shared a long stare at one another. Vultures can smell carrion from miles away. What had drawn this one to my house?

"Go away," I said. "Nobody's dead yet." I settled on the porch swing, listening for sounds from the gully, and trying to worry out an answer about what was going on in our usually peaceful hamlet.

I suppose I might have drifted off, because the gravel crunching when Diego pulled into the driveway at close to two in the morning awakened me. Alex stumbled in from the passenger seat and collapsed onto the sofa in the living room. Diego went straight to their bedroom and began methodically searching. As I had feared, he seemed pretty grumpy, so I tried to stay out of the way.

Luckily, he emerged fifteen minutes or so later to announce that all of their belongings were present and accounted for. I sent him outside with the flashlight to see if he could spot a body amidst the rubble of the now-lost front porch. He returned five minutes later with no news. All we could do was wait for daylight.

In any case, my family was now safely tucked in at home, and that was all it took for the dogs and me to tuck ourselves into our beds and fall fitfully asleep for what was left of the night.

You might think that would be more than enough excitement for Arroyo Loco for one week, but apparently the gods do not share that sentiment. I was hardly awake Monday morning, in my bathrobe and scuffs, my hair all askew, and standing at the kitchen sink filling the coffee carafe, when Bryce appeared and popped his dog Tippy inside my screened porch.

He caught sight of me through the window and called, not nearly as loudly as usual, "Oh, God, Estela, you'd better come quick this time. Chris says one of his kids found a body in the park! Hurry!" Bryce typically looks like a guy who doesn't get enough sun, but even through the window glass I could see he was especially pale this early morning, and his cheeks were blotched with red. He leapt off the porch steps and narrowly avoided trampling right through my new garden in his race to see what was happening at the park.

I stepped back to gather my thoughts as Diego and Alex emerged, freshly showered and half-prepared for their day at work.

"A body?" Alex said

I shook my head. "That's what Bryce said, but with him you can never be entirely sure. He said one of Chris' boys claims to have found a body in the park."

"Are you going down there?" Diego asked.

I gestured at my disheveled appearance. "Not like this, I'm not. I guess I'll go put some shoes on." I am not the world's fastest waker-upper, but shoes did seem like a good idea.

"I'll go," Diego said. Quickly wiping the last of the shaving cream from his chin and tossing the towel aside, he was gone in a flash.

The kitchen door had not swung fully shut before blood-curdling screams rang out from the Bantam's home across the road. "Alice!" I said. "Something's wrong with Alice!"

Her head still turbanned in a towel, Alex said, "I'll go see what's wrong!" and off she went.

I never move too fast, but I did manage to get some clothes on and out the door in what had to be record time. I stopped on the porch long enough to slip into some crocs I found there. Red crocs, in fact. Hmm. I've heard there have been some problems in town with those red Jump Bikes, and recently some Jump Scooters have appeared, but I've never heard of Jump Crocs. Still, there they were, and I needed some shoes. I let Tippy into the backyard with my dogs. Which way to go, then? To the park to gawk at a body or to the Bantams to help out with whatever trouble had erupted there?

A fresh set of multiple screams sent me dashing across the road. In addition to the cries, a wailing siren sounded as I climbed the flight of steps leading to the Bantam's front entrance. I clapped hands over my ears and pushed inside. Both Alex and Alice were yelling, a beeping alarm emanated from somewhere deeper in the house, and over it all, the siren continued to wail.

"Turn it off!" Alex yelled, pointing at the keypad mounted beside the door.

"I don't know how to turn it off!" Alice screamed back. "I don't know the code! You have to have a code! Ernie has the code!"

I glanced into a couple of rooms, but saw no signs of Ernie. "Where is Ernie?" I yelled. Since he's been confined to a wheelchair for several months, I knew he couldn't be far away. "Where's Ernie?"

"I don't know!" Alice's wails harmonized badly with the siren, the beeping alarm setting up a discordant back beat.

The only course of action that made any sense was to get out of there. I quickly ascertained that Ernie was nowhere to be found inside the house, although I did find his wheelchair parked in a corner of the darkened bedroom. It looked kind of lonesome sitting there. "Alex, let's get her out of here." At the sound of my voice, the ceiling fan overhead began whirling. It was as though the house was haunted by a mad scientist. I ran toward the front door and turned. "Alex, come on!" and the television came to life in the living room. Alice and Alex stumbled toward me, both now holding hands over their ears. I pulled open the door in anticipation of our escape and whacked my knee against a small table there. A brown package sat atop the table. Something eerie about the package stopped me, then I realized my name was on the address label. What was a package mailed to me doing in the Bantam's house? No time to wonder, I scooped it under one arm, and between us Alex and I guided Alice down her stairs and across to my house. The cacophony continued even as we left it behind. At least we were out of it and I could think.

CHAPTER SEVENTEEN

We plopped Alice on the porch swing and took a breather.

"Yes, yes," Alice kept saying, trying to get enough air in her lungs to complete a sentence. "Yes, it's all of those devices, you know? Ernie loves to fiddle with those devices. He has everything all connected some way."

Alex nodded. "You mean like the Nest? Your house is connected to Ernie's phone?"

"Yes, yes, something like that. I don't know what all. Ernie presses buttons and things go on and off, or he tells that Alexa box. I don't even know how to change the channel on the television any more. He showed me how the doorbell takes your picture. The fan, you know, in the ceiling, it comes on whenever. It's enough to drive an old woman to the funny farm, I can tell you." Alice heaved a deep sigh. "And now where is he? Bryce banged on our bedroom door, then went running, but Ernie wasn't in bed. I got up and looked, but couldn't find him anywhere."

Alex and I shared a glance. A body in the park, and Ernie missing? I hoped it wasn't what it was beginning to sound like.

"Try not to worry," I said. "Bryce and Diego went to look for him." That was sort of a falsehood, since both had headed to the park to check out the report of a body. With Ernie missing and a body found, it didn't take a rocket scientist to figure out there might be a connection. Still, no point in upsetting Alice with the possibility.

"Ernie can't go out without his wheelchair, you know?" Alice peered at me, the question in her eyes. "Where could he be?"

I patted her hand, smiled, and nodded. Really , what else could I do? Then I took a deep breath and looked at the package resting in my lap. Clearly addressed to me, it had somehow found its way inside Ernie's house. From the return address I could see it was likely the replacement part I had ordered for my blender. Possibly Arroyo Loco did have a package pirate, and possibly he was one of our own neighbors. Of course, Alice and Bryce also live in that house, so the pirate might not necessarily be the wheelchair-bound Ernie. If, in fact, the package had been stolen at all, and not simply delivered to the wrong address.

Alex turned her head, listening intently to voices drifting up the hill. Impossible to hear the words, but something was happening down that way. "We should go see … " She hesitated and gestured vaguely in the downhill direction. I cut a quick glance at Alice who stared in consternation at her own house, its alarms still blaring.

"Say, Alice," I said, trying to sound encouraging. "How about if we go to Freda's? You can stay with her, and Alex and I will go find Ernie for you." Freda and Alice are great friends, and they love a chance to get together for a visit.

"Yes, yes," Alice said, "but what about … " Her hands fluttered over her rumpled bathrobe. "Yes, yes," she said again, but didn't go on. I decided to take that to mean agreement with the plan. Maybe Freda could lend Alice one of her muumuus. I double-checked that the dog doors were open, the new gate securely locked, and turned the porch latch behind us as we left.

The three of us started off to Freda's, Alice continuing her chatter about Ernie's projects around the house. "Yes, you know, he has four different remote controls, and each one operates something different. That Alexa thing can turn on the television when he tells it, and he's always experimenting and changing things. I don't know how to work anything anymore, and then he goes and changes it anyway. Sometimes I think he wishes he had a remote to control me!"

Freda stood in her driveway peering toward the park as we arrived, but she quickly put an arm over Alice's shoulder and the two of them hurried inside. Freda threw me a few looks that I'm sure were meant to be meaningful and at one point jerked her head to the side, but I'm not adept at reading such enigmatic clues. I lowered my brow in a question, but she shook me off and bent to tune in to Alice's chatter.

I shrugged at Alex and we continued on toward the park where a gaggle of neighbors gathered at the edge, all of them staring at what appeared to be a bundle of old clothes on the ground about thirty feet away. I guessed the bundle would be the aforementioned dead body. I was quickly disabused of this gruesome notion when the bundle twitched and moaned. The tortured words were inaudible from where I had stopped, but several neighbors standing closer stepped quickly back, exchanging horrified looks. Alex and I crept closer.

I slipped up behind Sunshine, who stood rooted about ten feet from the moaning bundle. "Is that Ernie?" I asked.

"Yes, it is Ernie but he can't talk. I think he's been conked on the head. We're not sure. Bryce is trying to talk to him."

I looked again and saw Bryce lying beside and several feet to the right of Ernie. Bryce's mouth was going a mile a minute, but Ernie showed no signs of paying any attention to his son.

Someone shifted and my gaze locked onto a golf club lying on the ground this side of Ernie, who at that point had become eerily quiet. The golf club looked like a nine iron to me. Either Ernie had been the one to take the nine iron out of Grant's trunk in the first place, or whoever had taken it had conked Ernie with it. At least that seemed to be what Sunshine was implying.

At that moment, Ernie's body twitched in a shaking tremble and he gave a half-shriek, half-moan. Instead of helping him, a couple of people backed even farther away. Raymond glanced at Sunshine, Alex, and I huddled behind him. With eyes averted, he came toward us.

"Why doesn't someone help Ernie get off the dirt?" I asked. I stared at the prone man again. "He looks miserable."

Raymond nodded slowly, pursing his lips. "Yeah, he's miserable, okay. When we first got here, he said he'd been tasered. Said he tripped, then somebody tasered him. Said it must have been a midget, 'cause he never saw the guy. Then said he musta fallen on the taser 'cause he hurts all over again ever' time he moves. Doesn't want anyone to touch him, and truth is, no one wants to go that close anyway. We're all standing here waiting on the ambulance."

By that time, Helen had seen us, and come over to join the group. "We think it was one of Chris's kids. Chris told us he had a taser and maybe one of the kids got ahold of it. He went home to check."

I decided to chance it, and ask the question no one was asking. "What was Ernie doing out here in the first place? His wheelchair is home in his bedroom. I saw it myself." I cut a look to Helen. She and I had inadvertently witnessed Ernie walking at his house without his wheelchair several months ago, so we'd had some suspicion that Ernie might not be quite as wheelchair-bound as he has made himself out to be. Neither of us had said anything to anyone about our sighting, mostly because we thought we must be wrong. We couldn't think of any good reason why Ernie would be pretending a disability with which he was not genuinely afflicted. He was already retired, and so wouldn't need to fake a disability in order to get out of going to work. He wasn't that sort of irresponsible guy anyway. So we'd both kind of forgotten what we had seen and hadn't talked about it since. Even with the evidence right in front of us, neither of us mentioned our suspicions about Ernie's ability to get around without that chair.

Helen took another long gaze in Ernie's direction. "We think ... see how that nine iron is there?" We all took another look and nodded. "Ernie told Raymond ... well, ... Ernie told Raymond he was following a guy prowling out here early this morning."

Raymond nodded his confirmation.

"Before dawn?" I said.

"Yes, before dawn," Helen said.

"So, you think it was our photo-sensitive neighbor, Gerald?"

"Yes, probably. That's what I think, anyway."

"So Ernie is tiptoeing after Gerald early this morning before dawn. Christopher has equipped himself with a taser gun which he keeps in an unsecured location. One of the kids finds the taser, follows Ernie who is following Gerald and, for reasons unknown, the kid zaps Ernie."

Helen nodded and at the same time, scrunched her forehead into a puzzled expression, as well she might.

"Why, Helen? Why would the kid zap his neighbor, Ernie? And who hit who with the nine iron, if, in fact, anyone hit anyone?"

Sunshine jumped in with a surprisingly plausible explanation. "These kids probably don't really even know Ernie," she said. "You know, because he's always in his wheelchair and, well, probably they didn't even recognize it was him walking in the dark."

"Yes," Helen agreed, "and Christopher has been making everyone anxious about bad guys and guns and self-defense, so his kids think it's okay to go shooting people. We should be thanking our lucky stars it was just a taser and not an AK47."

About then, Ernie gave out with another loud moan. I decided it was time to hear the story from the horse's mouth, so to speak. If Ernie could moan, he could talk. I crept slowly toward his body, talking in as calm and comforting a tone as I would if approaching any other injured animal. From the ground on his other side, Bryce looked at me as a tear trickled across his dusty cheek.

I continued talking to Ernie, and he continued to moan, clearly in some serious pain. "Can you tell me where it hurts, Ernie? Maybe point to it?" Ernie was having trouble moving in any kind of coordinated way, but he did try to whisper. I leaned in closer, squatting next to his head. "What? What did you say, Ernie? Where does it hurt?"

He flapped one hand in the direction of his lower leg and whispered again. "My ankle. I think it's broken. My neck," Ernie moaned. "My neck. I can't move." He ran out of air and stopped talking.

Bryce and I stared at the sock covering Ernie's left ankle. The whole lower leg looked swollen to me. If the ankle wasn't broken, it was at least badly sprained. My eyes shifted focus and I saw what had likely caused that problem. A large gopher hole gaped a few inches from Ernie's sneaker. In the darkness, Ernie had very likely stepped right into that hole, twisted his ankle, and fallen to the ground. Hard to see how that sort of a fall had injured his neck, though, unless his neck snapped when he hit the ground, or he had fallen onto something.

I told Ernie he was absolutely right about his ankle, and rather than upsetting him, the news seemed to reassure him.

"The ambulance is coming, Dad," Bryce added.

"Wouldn't you like to try to sit up?" I asked. "Just roll over and we'll help you sit."

"No!" Ernie started to answer with a moan, but his reply quickly escalated to a hysterical shriek. "No! No! Oww! It's starting again!" Using the palm of his hand, he pushed his right shoulder off the ground an inch or so, still screaming.

"Is it the taser, Ernie?" I raised my voice to be heard over his wails.

At the same time, Bryce yelled, "There's something under there! A bug! There's a thing on his neck! Get it off, Estela! Get it off!"

I had already reared back on my haunches and mostly fallen backward. How did I get chosen to be the knight in shining armor for the day? I hate bugs, especially big stinging and excruciatingly painful bugs. Why didn't Bryce pull the bug off himself? Ernie was, after all, Bryce's father, and Bryce was already over on that side where he could see the thing, whatever it was.

I glared at Bryce, and he glared right back. "Help me turn him over," he said. I pulled at Ernie's hip, staying as far away as possible from Ernie's alleged bug-infested top half. Bryce pushed on his father's shoulder, and between us we rolled Ernie face up, his head coming right along with his body as though his neck was paralyzed in place. There was indeed a huge wasp-type bug stuck to his neck. One of the bright red wings was crumpled and broken and the whole creature looked sort of crushed. One leg waved feebly as though the wasp was taking its leave, then the thing fell off Ernie and lay still in the dirt.

"It's dead!" Bryce said.

This declaration was misunderstood by several, as I heard someone behind me exclaim, "Ernie's dead?" I felt the presence of bodies gathering closer to me as the others joined in the macabre human ritual of staring at the scene of a disaster. Ernie chose that moment to grind his teeth and moan, causing his audience to gasp and stumble backward again.

"Look at his neck!" Bryce said, pointing at Ernie's swollen neck. Purple hot flesh surrounded at least three distinct sting marks.

I didn't pay much attention to the movements and reactions of my neighbors, as I was too busy studying that now-dead bug. At least three inches long. A large, shiny black abdomen with splotches of bright blue. Translucent blood red wings, now broken.

"I know what that is," I said. "That's a tarantula hawk." More gasps, more hands going to mouths. I had to admit, just the name of that type of wasp is enough to terrify many people. And that's before they even know the damage a tarantula wasp can cause any human body that should happen to interfere with it.

"A tarantula!" Bryce said, leaping to his feet and prancing backward.

I couldn't move my eyes. "No, Bryce," I said. "That wasp is called a tarantula hawk. Although, now that you mention it, that wasp wouldn't be here if there wasn't a tarantula spider somewhere nearby. I sure hope that ambulance is coming soon." I took my eyes off the wasp and searched the surrounding dirt. "Look, see? That hole in the ground? Right there where Ernie fell. There's probably a tarantula in there. This wasp was probably hovering, trying to lure the spider out of the hole, when Ernie tripped on that other hole, the gopher hole by his foot, and fell on top of the wasp."

That was enough for a couple of the neighbors. Sunshine and Christopher scampered across the road and onto the paved sidewalk where any approaching tarantula could be spotted well in advance. Helen drew in closer to get a better look.

"See, she stung him at least three times," I said. "I've heard one sting is more painful than being tasered, and can instantly paralyze a human for several minutes. That wasp stung Ernie three times, and right on his neck where the swelling might … " I rocked back on my heels and looked at the remaining gawkers. "I just hope that ambulance gets here quickly. Somebody should call again. I don't even hear it coming." As an afterthought I added, "Does anyone happen to have an epipen handy?" We would need a quick way to reduce that swelling if it became impossible for Ernie to breathe. Even now, he was sucking hard to get air.

"Are there more of those hawks?" Bryce called from fifteen or twenty feet away, where he had retreated. Suddenly everyone started firing fearful glances at the ground nearby, searching for more wasps.

"Maybe," I said. "But tarantula hawks normally avoid humans. They hunt tarantulas. When they find one, they lure it out of its hole, then use their sting to paralyze the spider. They lay their egg on the tarantula's abdomen. The spider stays alive, but paralyzed, while the egg matures. The egg hatches and the larva eats the spider, eventually killing it." My explanation was followed by a horrified silence. Good to know those mornings spent at the local natural history museum were not wasted. Still, I may have gone into unnecessarily ghastly detail.

"Anyway," I said in a shaky voice, "it looks like Ernie face-planted on top of this one before she could lay her egg. I hear that, to humans, the sting is fiercely electric." I turned to those behind me and discovered that Helen was the only one there. The remainder of the small crowd had joined Sunshine across the road, and Raymond stood about ten feet away, bent over his phone. I hoped he was checking on the ambulance, and not doing further research on the life-cycle of the tarantula wasp. Beside me, Helen leaned in close for a better look.

"Oh. My. God. Did that wasp lay eggs inside of Ernie? Are they going to eat him from the inside out?" Helen, always with the cheerful thoughts. "Can surgeons get it out? The poor tarantula!"

I peered at the red puncture marks. Larger than a pin would make. Smaller than a hole that might be made by an ice pick. The holes looked to be about the same size as the wound left in my arm in the fifth grade when Ricardo Amato, for almost no provocation, stabbed me with his geometry compass, the kind with a pencil on one leg and a dangerously sharp metal point on the other. Even more painful than the stab with the compass was the tetanus shot the school nurse made me get. Anyway, Ernie's punctures looked plenty big enough to have had a wasp egg inserted inside by a determined ovipositor.

His jaws still tightly clenched, Ernie pulled his hands to his chest and emitted more long, loud moans. Too late, I realized it might have been better if I had not gone into such detail within his earshot. Still, it did not look as though Ernie was engaging at all with anything beyond his own pain-racked body.

We finally heard the wailing siren of the ambulance as it traveled the winding highway toward Arroyo Loco. The EMTs did not appear to have ever encountered a victim of multiple tarantula hawk stings before. They went about bundling Ernie onto a gurney in an efficient manner anyway. At the last minute I persuaded one of them to scoop the dead wasp into a paper cup. No way to know if an emergency room doctor would know what to do for Ernie, but at least they would know exactly what was wrong with him.

CHAPTER EIGHTEEN

Bryce, always a stalwart and devoted son, whimpered uncontrollably as the EMTs loaded Ernie for transport, so Raymond climbed in the back to accompany his friend to the hospital. I sent one of the kids to Freda's to let Alice know that Ernie was not dead after all. At least not yet.

Several folks lingered, most still in a gaggle across the road. Helen peered curiously down the presumed tarantula hole, probably waiting for its occupant to make an appearance. My guess was the lucky spider within had lived through her near miss with a horrible death, and would go on to do her part to continue to populate our canyon with her feared but generally harmless offspring. On another note, I wondered if this tarantula, tarantula hawk, and gopher hole infested park might not be the best place to let children play.

Having carefully inspected the spider hole, Helen trotted toward the small gathering that included Sunshine. I recognized that nasty glint in Helen's eye, and called her back. "Helen!" I knew her too well.

She stopped and looked my way. I walked closer, and said quietly, "How about if we don't say anything to Sunshine about the possible wasp egg inside Ernie?"

She sputtered. "But, but, 'Stel', that's the best part, and it's all true, right? Ooh, that's really gonna freak Sunshine!"

"Yes, Helen, it probably would really upset Sunshine and a few others. Why would you want to scare everyone?"

She lowered her brow and glared at me, but I could see she knew I was right. "Oh, all right," she grumbled. "I won't say anything."

A little sorry to have spoiled her fun, I patted her arm. Bryce joined us and the three of us walked toward the group.

"Hey, guess what?" Bryce said when we got there. "Estela says that wasp laid her eggs inside my dad." He cut a sideways glance to me and snickered. I restrained my impulse to slap him. He probably thought it was funny because he didn't really believe it could be true.

From his other side, Helen felt no such compunction to restrain herself. She punched him hard in the shoulder. "Shut up, Bryce."

"Ow!"

I pulled Bryce aside while he rubbed his shoulder and whined. "So, Bryce, do you have any idea why your dad was creeping through Arroyo Loco before dawn this morning? There've been a lot of strange things happening here lately. Was Ernie up to no good?"

Bryce puffed his chest for a second, as though he was thinking about being indignant, but then he deflated. Ever the ingratiating orator, Bryce said, "Don't be stupid, Estela. Dad was trying to stop trouble, not start it. He knew about all the stuff going on here. He wanted to find whoever was doing it."

Helen joined us. "So, what about Ernie walking, Bryce? We're all supposed to think he's confined to a wheelchair, and here he is walking all the way down here at the park. What's going on with that?"

Bryce rubbed his shoulder again and gazed along the canyon. "It is possible he had a miraculous recovery. Mom's been praying every night. Possibly her prayers were finally answered."

I caught Helen's glance behind Bryce's back. Both of us suppressed eye rolls. "Bryce," I said, "Ernie can walk, though, right? And before you answer, you should know that both Helen and I have seen Ernie walking."

Still not making eye contact, and in a small voice, Bryce said, "Possibly. At home, where he has lots of things to hold onto." He turned to face us again, his lips tightened into an almost invisible line, his voice a high whine. "But if you guys have seen him walking then you know more than I do. Why are you even asking me? I'm telling you, if my dad was out here walking, he was trying to stop trouble, not start it."

Here it was eight o'clock in the morning and I was already too tired to argue with Bryce. Besides, I wasn't in a position to know one way or the other. All I could think was, wow, there sure are a lot of folks rambling through Arroyo Loco at night, and most of them have completely eluded my radar.

When we turned to the rest of the group, the discussion was about mounting a campaign to eradicate the tarantulas. I pointed out that the tarantula is native to the semi-arid environs of Arroyo Loco, and shared a few more factoids garnered from my trips to the museum, including how tarantulas are an important part of a healthy ecosystem. I got blank stares to my contributions. Undeterred, I went on to explain that tarantulas eat baby rattlesnakes and lots of other beetles, bugs, and spiders. This news was greeted with more sympathetic mumbles.

I grabbed Bryce's elbow and dragged him up the hill with Helen trailing along behind. When we got to Freda's, I sent Bryce inside to collect his mother so the two of them could get themselves to the hospital. Even if Ernie wouldn't be allowed to come home later today, Raymond would still need a ride back to Arroyo Loco. Diego and Alex waved from their Prius as they passed, finally on their way to work.

Helen lingered beside me, and after everyone else had gone out of earshot, she pulled me closer. "So what about this Ernie walking out here, 'Stel'? Doesn't it seem kind of obvious he's the one doing all this mischief and mayhem? I mean, sure, that Gerald kid swiped Freda's tomatoes, but the rest of it had to be Ernie, right?"

"I don't know, Helen. Why would Ernie pry mailboxes off the wall? Why would Ernie take Nina's house key from under her potted geranium? What's his motive?"

Helen lowered her brow and gazed into space, contemplating. After a bit, she said, "Stirring up trouble?"

I thought about that. Maybe, surprisingly, that suggestion was not entirely out of character for Ernie, but he would have to have a good reason to want to cause trouble in his own neighborhood. I thought of something else. "Does it seem to you like most of the more serious mischief is happening closer to the highway? You know, at that end of the canyon?"

Helen nodded slowly, still gazing into space.

I went on, thinking out loud. "For the sake of argument, let's say it is Ernie, and let's say he's doing it intentionally, to cause trouble. He's causing the trouble at the roadhouse, at Nina's and Graciela's, places at that end of the canyon. Now think about motive. What is he trying to get done?"

Helen's brow scrunched even deeper, she squinted her eyes and shook her head at me in confusion. No enlightenment coming from that quarter, I guessed. I'd had some thoughts, but decided to table them for now. Even if I was right, being the bearer of unwelcome news is never a good place to be.

I bid her farewell and continued on to my now-quiet home, poured myself a bowl of cornflakes, and parked on the porch swing to contemplate the events of this short but already busy day. Six or eight tiny brown birds splashed in the birdbath, chattering noisily. I considered grabbing my new field guide and binoculars, then decided instead to let my mind wander where it would and see if I could solve these crimes in Arroyo Loco. Evidently where it wanted to wander was back to sleep, because sometime later I was startled awake by the sound of Nina swinging open the creaking porch screened door.

She slid into the worn wicker chair across from me, the scent of the previous evening's cloying perfume wafting between us. I realized then that Nina had not been among those gathered at the scene of Ernie's accident this morning. Probably still staying somewhere in the safety of town, and from the fragrance of it, not alone.

She demanded to be told the whole story. I did some judicious editing, and made it clear the situation did not warrant any greater degree of fear than she already felt. Other than that, she got the truth, at least most of the truth.

"So, Nina," I said when I was through, "what do you think Ernie was doing down at the park before dawn? He's not usually a brave law-enforcer type of guy."

"No, he's not. He's more of a techie guy. You know, how he's always trying to get us to install cameras here and there?"

"Oh, brother. Speaking of that, you should see what he's got installed all over his house. A doorbell that takes your picture. Ceiling fans that go on and off on command. Alice says she can't even figure out how to change channels on the television any more. When I was there, I stepped into their kitchen and something started making a noise. I think it was the coffee grinder."

Nina gave a hollow laugh and shook her head. "Remember when he wanted us to install a gate across the road?"

"Oh, yes! I'd forgotten about that. You know, I think you might be onto something. What if Ernie is doing some of this mischief to persuade us to install those cameras, or go back to that gate idea? Is that possible?"

"I can see him possibly spray-painting Graciela's fence. If we had cameras mounted there we could have seen whoever did that."

"Yes! We might really be onto something here." I nodded encouragingly to Nina. Maybe I could convince her to be the neighborhood bearer of unwelcome news.

"But what about the mailboxes, Estela? As Bryce keeps telling us, that was a federal crime. Would Ernie really try something like that just to scare us?"

"You have a point. He might not even be strong enough to do that kind of damage, even using that golf club as a pry bar. Still, he might be responsible for some of our mischief. So, what? Gerald is doing some of the stuff, Ernie is doing other things, and some of what's happening is being done by someone else? It does seem like the more serious stuff, break-ins, thievery, and so on, has to be being done by someone other than Gerald or Ernie."

Nina nodded. "I know you think I'm a wimp, Estela, but I'm going to finish running a load of laundry and then I'm headed back to work, and to stay in town again for the night. Whatever is going on, this place is too scary for me." With that, she stood and started home. If she had said Arroyo Loco was a dangerous place, I might have argued with her. Instead, she'd said she was scared and there's no sense in arguing that it's not too scary. Scary, like so many other feelings, is in the eye of the beholder.

I carried my dishes inside, which was when I noticed the tiny light on my landline answering machine blinking. Muñoz had left a message about scheduling a Neighborhood Watch group. He opined that might be a better solution than folks arming themselves with golf clubs, tasers, and guns. I wondered out loud about who might have been the one to spill the beans to the detective about all of those goings on.

I called the number Muñoz left, which turned out to be the direct line to the officer who scheduled the Neighborhood Watch meetings. We had a nice chat and discussed our specific needs here in Arroyo Loco. The Watch meetings were scheduling out into October, so I picked a random evening, thinking we'd have plenty of time to get the word out. She cheerily informed me that the officer who met with us would bring many important resources, including those nifty window stickers identifying each home as being part of the our Neighborhood Watch group. As an afterthought, I asked about window stickers informing emergency responders about how many and what sort of pets lived inside each home, but apparently that wasn't part of her jurisdiction.

Still thinking about pets after I disconnected, I considered the possibility of spending a few minutes practicing nose work with the dogs. Honestly, if I would just do the practice when I think about it, instead of thinking about practicing and then feeling guilty when I don't, I would probably be a significantly more effective person. Not to mention my dogs would know how to use their noses better.

Sitting still long enough set me back to thinking about neighbors watching out and nocturnal wanderings. It did seem that the list of mischief and mayhem we had suffered could be roughly divided into three categories, those being events most likely attributable to Gerald, those possibly caused by Ernie, and a third category of events more malicious in nature and likely not caused by either Gerald or Ernie.

On a whim, I hit the speed dial to Muñoz. My call was forwarded to his office in the sheriff's substation, where he was "not in at the present time." My question was an easy one, so I asked the woman who had answered. As I suspected, having heard nothing more on the news since yesterday, the prison inmate who had disappeared while being transferred to the mental hospital had not been re-captured. His whereabouts remained unknown. I disconnected and sat back.

Someone had stolen clothing, a large beach towel, and food items. Someone had also tried to get into our mailboxes. I wasn't sure if that fit the picture that was forming. Sure, one grandchild here in Arroyo Loco might be expecting a birthday card containing a small amount of cash, but that seemed so unlikely. Would someone really pry mailboxes open on the off-chance there might be ten dollars in an envelope?

What was I thinking here? Even if the inmate had ridden to our town as a stowaway in the trunk of Grant's car, how could he still be hanging around? Then again, we'd all become so wary this week that even those of us who did not normally lock our cars had been religious about doing so. If the inmate had tried to steal a car, he hadn't had any luck yet. And even if he changed his appearance dramatically, hitchhiking on the highway would be risky at best. I had to at least consider the possibility that dratted inmate was hiding somewhere nearby.

Although, Arroyo Loco harbored oodles of possible hiding places, all of those had been searched, some of them repeatedly, and we had all been vigilantly on the lookout for days. Another search party would likely be as fruitless as the others. Even the big house at the top of the hill, which presented itself as a likely hiding spot, had at least had its perimeter thoroughly scoured without any luck. I couldn't think of anyplace that had not already been searched.

This did not mean the escaped inmate was not still hiding somewhere nearby. Unless we tried something different, future searches would be as unsuccessful as had the previous ones. But what should we do differently?

Memories about the system of deer trails crisscrossing these hills flitted through my mind. The trails themselves would not afford a suitable place to hide, since they were frequented by a variety of wildlife from boars, to coyotes, to our own teenagers escaping imperious parents. However, there were hiding places accessible on that trail system. Easily climbed giant valley oaks might provide an arboreal hiding place. Granite boulders left tumbled about the hillsides sometimes formed cavities among them where a person might hide. In fact, as I thought about it, I did remember a cave-like place I had once seen over the hill from my own house.

Maybe, I thought, I should track down the teenagers. If those girls, or any of the other kids, had been out on those trails they might possibly have seen something suspicious, other than just the light on at Amanita's. I tried to call Randy, most often the leader of our indigenous pack of kids. I got his mother instead, given that I was calling the landline in their house. As it turned out, I had failed to factor in that Randy and his peers were now young men, and they were either away at college or, in Randy's case, in town at work and getting ready to ship out for basic training in Texas. His mother assured me the boys had not been out on the trails for a year or more, although how she could be sure of that I had to wonder. I decided not to share that I had recently heard her daughter Colleen, who must be thirteen or so by now, had been out on that trail only a day or so before. Kids get ratted on enough without a whole village of nosy neighbors tattling on them.

Back to Square One. Shiner chose that moment to drop one of his numerous squeaky toys in my lap. The poor dog was bored, and one never wants to let a border collie go too long without a task. The story is, if you don't give a border collie a job, he'll invent one for himself, and it might be a job you don't want done, such as digging up and murdering every single one of your precious bearded iris rhizomes in a single afternoon. But I digress.

Grumbling, I stood and started gathering the boxes and scent items for a nose work practice session. Both dogs love the nose work game so much, I had to shut one dog at a time inside so I could practice with the other one without interference. Each dog had a couple of successful practice searches followed by treats and a short game of fetch in the backyard.

It wasn't until I returned to my chair that the obvious dawned on me. If Shiner could reliably find the faint scent of cloves in one of eight identical cardboard boxes and show me an alert, maybe he really could follow the smell of an escaped inmate from the trunk of the car where the bad guy had possibly stowed away to his current hiding place. It was at least worth a try, and what an exciting way to test our tracking skills.

CHAPTER NINETEEN

Perhaps having more faith in Shiner's scenting ability than was warranted, I nevertheless quickly leashed both dogs and got ready to go looking for the stowaway. Then I stopped and went back for my sturdy shoes. No telling where this search might lead, and I didn't want to be stymied by inappropriate footwear. I'd almost made it the door when I had another thought and headed back to the closet.

I had to rummage around in there for a bit, but I finally came up with my not-so-lucky Giants baseball cap with the nine millimeter bullet hole shot clean through the brim. I whacked it couple of time on my leg to dislodge some of the dust, then stuffed it down over my curls. I was ready. The three of us hurried to Helen's house to collect scent from the trunk of Grant's Buick.

Of course, this being Monday and Grant being at work, the Buick was not in the driveway. An unfamiliar silver sedan sat in its place. In fact, Helen informed me when I knocked, the Buick was at that moment locked inside the sheriff's impound yard being inspected for evidence to determine if the inmate had in fact ever been inside that vehicle.

"Rats," I said, and explained my plan.

Keeping her screened door tightly latched, Helen stared dubiously at the dogs milling at my feet. "Can't you just tell them, 'search' or something?"

"I could, but how are they supposed to know what to search for, Helen? It'd be like if I said to you, 'go get that.' You'd have no idea what to get."

She squinted at me again. I wondered if she might be developing a tic of some kind, at least in that one eye. "They're border collies, right? Aren't border collies supposed to be so smart? I saw this one on television a while back who knew the names of more than a hundred toys."

"So you think if I said, 'search for the escaped inmate' my dogs would know what to do?"

"Now, Estela, there's no need to use that tone." She slammed her front door closed.

I was immediately sorry I'd alienated her. Nothing was to be gained from letting my frustration get to me. I scanned the canyon from Helen's front porch. If I couldn't get the inmate's scent from Grant's Buick, where else might I get it? What else might he have touched that would retain his smell? Even Diego's Prius was gone today, and it didn't seem likely the mailboxes would still smell like the person who had pried at them. Too many other humans had swarmed over them since Saturday morning. Although many of us believed at least some of the mischief happening in Arroyo Loco had likely been caused by this escaped inmate, no one really knew that to be true, or if he was even still here somewhere.

Then it sort of dawned on me, wasn't that really the point? We didn't know if he was still hiding nearby, and my earlier thought had been that he might be somewhere along that deer trail system meandering over the hills. If I took my dogs out for a nice stroll along those trails, I was quite certain they would locate any other human out there. Both of my guys are very friendly, and always looking for someone, anyone, who might potentially throw a ball for them. Instead of giving the dogs a target scent and formally tracking a particular individual, we'd simply go for a walk and see what, or who, we could see. Or rather, smell what they could smell. The time had come to search where dogs could smell, instead of looking where humans could see.

In case there might still be some scent there to trigger Shiner's nose, I let him sniff the ground near where the Buick had been parked last week. The spot was still identified by a few crumbles of auto glass lying amongst the gravel.

The three of us accessed the trail by climbing the hill behind the Raskin's house, the same way I had right after the previous house on that lot had burned down a couple of years ago. The dirt-floored clearing surrounded by small boulders was still there on the hillside, although it did not show any signs of having been occupied recently. I stepped to where the trail started uphill from there and tried to solicit Shiner's attention to the dust.

"Here, Shiner, here." I pointed at the ground, hoping he would get the idea and take a whiff of anyone who might have passed lately. He gave no sign of understanding my intent. "Here, right here!" Scout came around from the other side and gazed at the ground also, but didn't sniff at it. They both made eye contact with me, clearly wishing to be cooperative, but confused.

"Okay, never mind. Let's go along here and sniff as we go." Which is what they did, and pretty much what they usually do when we walk. Scout caught the scent of something first, at the base of a small bush. His nose carried him deeper under the bush where nothing larger than a mouse could be hiding. He was on the scent of something, certainly, but not anything that would interest his human.

We continued on in this way for a half an hour or more, catching scents on what looked like rabbit trails, prickly bushes where tufts of what looked suspiciously like cat fur were caught, and even one flat rock where a fox or coyote had left their scat. Clearly, any scent that interested dogs was not the same scent I was hoping to find and follow.

It wasn't until then that I fully realized what kind of danger might lurk ahead. Sure, the dogs and I were having fun checking out all the scents along the trail, and even if we found humans they would probably be no more sinister than a small gaggle of teenage girls. Still, there was the escaped prisoner to think about. He might really be out here. It was the thought of the girls that kept me going. If they were out on this hillside, we'd better at least check and make sure the dangerous inmate was not nearby. On the other hand, what I would do if it turned out he was nearby?

The dogs and I reached that place just over the hill where three granite boulders, each bigger than a car, had tumbled into one another, forming at their bases the entrance to a cave of indeterminate depth. I paused for a few deep breaths and to consider the situation, then realized that, yet again, I had gotten myself into a predicament from which the only way was forward. Shiner stared at that hole and gave a high whine, clearly indicating that something, or someone was inside.

The opening was so narrow. A child might squeeze through that hole. It was harder to imagine a full-grown adult man getting inside. Still, Shiner stared. I have learned to trust my dogs. When they indicate that something, or someone, is present, even if I can't see anyone, I know the dogs are right. I crept closer, Shiner at my heels. I leaned over for a better look. Both dogs sniffed excitedly at the entrance. I had a moment of concern, not wanting to discover the occupied den of some annoyed woodland creature, but the absence of animal tracks in the dust near the entrance alleviated that particular concern.

Shiner looked at me and whined. Both dogs crowded close to my head. Before I could move, they started a cacophony of their loudest, most threatening barks, temporarily deafening me. Someone was definitely in residence inside. Once again, my dogs had saved the day. Sort of. What should I do next, now that they had found this guy?

I pulled the dogs away long enough to lean over and peer as far as I could into the back reaches of the cave, wishing I had thought to equip myself with a flashlight. As my eyes slowly adjusted to the dim light inside, objects came into focus. About three feet back, the edge of an aluminum soda can caught what little light penetrated. Something moved and I heard an accompanying scraping sound.

I rolled back on my heels and thought about what to do. I am a psychotherapist, and the individual now trapped inside this small cave was pinned there by two vicious-sounding dogs. Maybe I should try talking the guy out? On the other hand, was it a good idea to let this individual, who might very well be a dangerous escaped prisoner, know that his captors were really a lone middle-aged lady and her two easy-going border collies? This guy had already gone to some serious trouble to escape from law enforcement. If he found out I was out here by myself, and I was not an armed sheriff's deputy with a sharp-toothed canine officer, what kind of danger would my dogs and I find ourselves in then?

I pulled out my cell phone, but discovered something I should have expected earlier. We all had cell service in the canyon because we had a wireless router mounted on the roof of the roadhouse. Here, the other side of the hill and a good half mile from the router, there was no cell service. I stared in frustration at the empty bars displayed on the device. I am one of those people who uses technology without having any real understanding of how it works. I tried to call Helen, but the phone didn't complete the call. I tried to think who was still in Arroyo Loco and might come to my rescue. I sent a text to Freda.

Help! I'm on the trail behind the Raskins

But the text never "delivered" Nothing.

More scrabbling sounds came from inside the cave. Was the guy twisting himself over, preparing to come out? I eased back, farther out of sight. Stared at my phone again, belatedly remembering it had a flashlight built into it somewhere. Not remembering how to access that feature. As far as I knew, the phone had no feature resembling a weapon of any kind.

Should I run back to the ridge top and yell for help? So many residents of Arroyo Loco had left, fearing for their safety, I couldn't be sure anyone would hear me. And those left behind were, for the most part, locked tightly in their homes. Not very likely any of them would hear me either.

This guy could probably easily catch me if I tried to run for it. Besides, in my haste I would certainly trip over my own dogs and fall, possibly suffering serious injuries from the fall alone. No telling what amount of damage would be done when the bad guy then caught up with me. My mind was spinning a mile a minute imagining no end of bad outcomes.

Maybe I should put the dogs in a "down-stay," run to get help myself, and hope seeing the dogs would scare the bad guy enough to keep him in his cave. Seriously? I had to chide myself. Does that sound like anything I would do? I wasn't leaving my dogs here with this dangerous criminal. And anyway, he'd have to crawl out to see them, and then he'd know I had left.

Maybe I should stay here and send Shiner back to fetch someone. Lassie used to do that sort of thing. She'd go back and signal rescuers to follow her by tipping her head. Regretfully, I've never taught that particular trick to either of my dogs. In fact, I'm pretty sure I would not even be able to persuade them to leave me here, let alone summon help.

Both dogs can herd sheep. Maybe I could use those skills to get some help. I could send Shiner out on a "get around." He would leave my side if I gave him that command, but then he'd circle the hill until he found something he could round up. No telling who or what that might be. It might be another human, but it would as likely be another dog, or a wayward sheep, or some other hapless creature. Possibly even a lost cat.

I set aside that idea. I'd probably been sitting there wondering what to do for at least twenty minutes by then. Why wasn't someone else coming to find me? What happened to all the busybodies and snoops in Arroyo Loco? If Lauren had been home, she would have seen me heading out this trail, but she and Kelly had gone to stay in town. If Betsy still lived here, for sure she would have come sneaking along to catch me at whatever mischief she thought I was up to here. Unlucky for me, to the best of my knowledge, Betsy still resided in Chowchilla Women's Prison as a guest of state taxpayers. No, this time I was on my own.

I went back to thinking about what might happen if I simply took my dogs and left, hoping the bad guy didn't follow me. On the other hand, now that I finally had the guy cornered, I was reluctant to let him get away. Who knows what he would do next if I let him escape again? I pulled out my phone and tried to connect another phone call. Still no luck. What a strange world where I couldn't just dial the phone I carried in my back pocket and summon help.

The dogs heard it before I did, and both tipped their heads toward the sound. I stopped moving and listened. Finally I heard it. A soft baying in the distance, growing louder, coming closer. That had to be Itches, Sunshine's beagle. She must have gotten out of their yard and, like any self-respecting hound would do, was headed to the hills in search of prey. Would she be attracted this direction if I called her name, or would she go the other way, thinking I was trying to catch her? Should I yell "help" instead? That would clue the bad guy that I was alone and helpless in the face of any attack he cared to mount.

On the other hand, he would still have to come scrabbling out of that cave, giving me some warning. I've noticed at previous scary junctures of my life that having some warning of approaching or imminent danger is somewhat over-rated. So you get the warning. Then what? Another few seconds in which to assume an even more effective cowering position?

Shiner solved my dilemma by barking twice. I have no idea what those barks communicated to Itches, if anything, but the baying did grow closer still.

Even better, now there was a babble of voices following behind Itches. Either someone had finally noticed my absence and come in search, or Sunshine and friends were trying to find Itches. In any case, a few seconds later the smallish brown and white dog with floppy ears burst into sight a few feet down the trail. All three dogs were apparently great friends, because they began wriggling in typical dog-greeting-dog behavior.

I scooted a few yards in their direction and met Helen and Sunshine as they trundled up in pursuit of Itches. I stopped them and put a finger to my lips.

"What? What?" Helen's loud whisper could probably be heard well inside the cave.

I scowled and hushed her. "He's in there," I said, pointing so as to avoid using too many words.

"Where?" Helen said, trying to peer around me in the direction I pointed.

I could have gone into a long explanation, but decided I didn't want to bother. Besides, by then Itches had developed a serious interest in the occupant of the cave and was snuffling loudly at the entrance. If I had been the bad guy, I might have been tempted to grab Itches' collar and try to use her as a hostage to get out of this pickle. Itches appeared to be oblivious to the danger, as she whined and snuffled, pushing deeper into the opening between the rocks.

"Sunshine," I said, figuring she was both the most dispensable human at the scene, and also the one least likely to become distracted from her mission, "Please, take Itches home, and when you get there, call Muñoz!" I whispered as loudly as I dared into her ear. If the bad guy heard that law enforcement was on its way, no telling what he would do. "Really fast, Sunshine. Here, use one of my leashes, take Itches home, and tell Muñoz it's an emergency. Get him out here fast! This really is an emergency!"

Sunshine's eyebrows shot skyward and her eyes grew round. She took the end of the leash I offered, clipped it to her dog, and started downhill as fast as she could go in her Birkenstocks, dragging Itches behind. That dog made herself a dead weight, not wanting to leave the exciting prey she had cornered in the rocks. Just before Sunshine disappeared, I called, "Hurry!"

Helen crept closer to the hole between the rocks. Both of my dogs followed her, burying their snouts inside. No one's tail wagged, so this was not a friendly incursion.

Another scrabbling inside spoke of the hidden man's mounting anxiety. Finally, he spoke.

"Get away from me!" he growled, and he may have kicked at the dogs, because they backed out fast. Shiner gave a couple of his angry barks aimed into the cave opening. Again, I was tempted to turn and run with the dogs away from the danger posed by a desperate criminal on the loose. Helen shifted closer to me and I clung to her arm.

"Who's out there?" the bad guy growled again when the barking stopped. "Who is out there? One woman, right? All by yourself, are you? You and your friendly dogs?" The scrabbling sounds inside the cave moved closer to the entrance. If he stuck his head out, he would see we were no threat at all.

"Oh, there's more than one of us," Helen said. The quaver in her voice gave away her fear. Her next words did not. "More than one of us. Two trained dogs, and my trusty nine millimeter Sig Sauer here." Helen made her empty hand into the shape of a gun and pointed her finger at the opening. "And my Sig is aimed right where your head will appear if you try to crawl out of there. Let me suggest you stay put for now. My trigger finger is feeling a bit jumpy." That last part was easy to believe because Helen's voice cracked into a whole different octave. She cleared her throat.

I felt slightly desperate myself. Fifteen minutes for Sunshine to get to her phone and make the call, thirty minutes for Muñoz or whoever was on duty to drive out here, and another ten to climb the trail to our location. Helen and I could easily be here for an hour trying to keep this guy from even so much as looking out and finding two scared people, two very friendly dogs, and no nine millimeter anything.

CHAPTER TWENTY

After having made a daring escape from prison, things had kind of been going downhill for this guy. The county was swarming with both law enforcement officers and the general public on the lookout for him, and he wasn't making much of a living here in Arroyo Loco. A few stolen sodas and an occasional pop-top can of beans weren't going to be enough to keep him going for much longer. Once he figured out we were no threat, he'd be out of there in a flash, and might even take one of us hostage. I eased slightly behind Helen. I was smaller, easier to grab and push around. It only made sense.

The scrabbling started up again, and the heels of some well-worn sneakers appeared closer to the cave entrance.

"I mean it!" Helen said. "I see so much as one hair on your head, I'm pulling this trigger!" I didn't have time to point out he seemed to be emerging feet, not head-first.

"Yeah, yeah, I get it," he said. Before I could breathe a sigh of relief, he added. "Tell you what. You shoot something else. A rock, a tree. Shoot something so I know you really got a gun, 'cause if you don't, I'm coming out."

Uh-oh. I checked my phone. Nine minutes had elapsed since Sunshine had shuffled away. Still most of an hour to wait. I leaned close to Helen's ear.

"Maybe we should quietly slip away? Now we know for sure the escapee is here, the sheriff can bring his whole crew in and search. This bad guy won't be able to get too far."

One of Helen's eyebrows had dropped, making her face a skeptical scowl. "But we have him trapped!" she whispered back. "Why would we let him go?"

I put my hand over my mouth and spoke even more quietly. "No, actually, he's not trapped at all. He could crawl out of there at any second. Then where would we be?"

Helen nodded slowly and began to scan our surroundings. I joined in her visual search. Maybe if we could locate a couple of good-sized rocks, we could hit him on the head if he tried to crawl out. I understood Helen's intent, but all things considered this did not seem like a wise plan. We would have to each stand close enough to the hole to hit him as he tried to crawl out, assuming his head came first. And we'd have to stand far enough back that he couldn't grab one of our ankles, pull us to the ground, and use our own rocks to inflict grievous, possibly even fatal injuries.

"So, what about it?" he said. "You shoot something or I'm coming out now."

"I'm not wasting bullets proving anything to you, buster." Considering she had nothing, Helen sounded quite convincing. She must have learned to talk like that in her job as a librarian at the state prison. She wasn't finished. "Every one of these bullets has your name on it. Go ahead, make my day. Stick your head out and I'll blow your brains away."

I checked my phone. Another six minutes gone. I listened for even a faint sound of an approaching siren, but all I heard were panting dogs. Even the birds in the canyon had gone silent.

The sounds of movement started again inside the hole. The whole bottom of the guy's worn sneakers appeared at the opening. He was coming out, but feet first. More movement and we could see white cotton socks.

"Here," Helen whispered. "Quick, give me that leash!"

I unclipped the last leash and handed it to her. She slipped the catch through the handle, making a wide slip-knot, and, like a rodeo cowgirl and with more courage that I could have mustered, she grabbed the guy by the ankles, slid the loop over his feet, and yanked it tight.

"Ow!" he hollered loud enough that his voice echoed through the canyon. Helen had really stirred up a wasp's nest now. Faster than I could have imagined, she whipped the rest of the leash around his ankles several more times, and secured the catch to the handle. She stepped back, one fist raised, like the cattle-ropers in the county fair. Wedged into the cave, unable to maneuver and with his ankles rendered immobile, our bad guy was all tied up. When law enforcement finally arrived, all they would have to do would be to haul him out by his feet.

Then, far in the distance, voices came this way again.

"Oh, cripes," Helen said. "Is that the whole crew coming up here?" Her tone seemed to indicate she was annoyed at what I was taking to be a hopeful prospect. I could imagine Helen picturing herself as the big hero, holding the escaped prison inmate trapped in his spider hole with only her hand pointing a finger-pistol at his head.

To Helen's dismay, a few moments later almost everyone still left in Arroyo Loco appeared tromping along the trail in a disorganized parade. Freda, as she is wont to do, serenaded the crew of hikers with a selection of Austrian favorites, including a rousing chorus from The Happy Wanderer in which a few others joined along. "Val-deri, Val-dera." When they got to the "ha ha ha ha" part, the two youngest hikers, looked like a couple of Christopher's boys, dissolved in hysterics. All very frightening to the trapped inmate, I'm sure.

While we're on the subject, who brings children along on an expedition to capture a dangerous criminal?

Once the general merriment had subsided, I scanned the crowd and asked if anyone had been left behind to give the sheriff's deputies directions to our location, and was assured Sunshine along with Christopher's oldest had volunteer to lead the deputies to the cave. Christopher himself strode bravely to the cave entrance and informed its occupant that he had "a powerful taser" pointed inside. At least Christopher's threat was not an empty one, as he really was in possession of his weapon.

The cavalry having arrived in the form of my neighbors, this seemed like an excellent time to gather my canine crew and scamper to the safety of home.

I turned to get my dogs' attention, and realized they were both staring intently at something high on the rock beside us. Sure enough, perched ten feet overhead and peering down at the curious scene we must have presented, was the escaped cat, Mocha. I wrestled on the horns of a dilemma. Should I let the cat out of the bag, so to speak, and call Helen's attention to the feline previously known as her cat, or leave the situation alone? Mocha looked well-fed and for all the world, as happy as a cat could be. He could not have appeared less in need of rescuing. Resolving to "let sleeping dogs lie" or something along those lines, I pushed the dogs' heads away from the overshadowing cat, and called them to follow without a word to Helen. Two dogs, zero leashes. I kept my fingers crossed that I wouldn't run into Amanita on the way home.

Several large vehicles, sirens blaring, pulled into Arroyo Loco just as my dogs and I made it out to the road. Law enforcement had arrived, and the escaped inmate and my neighbors and friends would all be safely relieved of their various predicaments by the time I'd gotten to my screened porch and had my feet parked on the hassock.

Out of sight of all the excitement, I had a chance to rest my eyes, count my blessings, and take a few deep breaths. Or it may have been many deep breaths, because the sun was in a whole different place when the squeal of the screened porch door and Helen's not-so-quiet footfalls caused me to open my eyes.

"Good golly Miss Molly!" she exclaimed, and plopped herself on the wicker across from me, slinging the six-pack of generic ginger ale she carried onto the hassock at my feet. "That was a thrill, wasn't it? You and I, we saved the day! Well, and your dogs, too."

Acknowledging the usefulness of my dogs in saving the day was an unusual concession for Helen to make. I nodded in agreement and laughed as both dogs burst through the dog door to greet our visitor, tails aloft.

"So everything worked out?" I said, "They caught the guy?"

"Yep! They made all of us leave the area while they got him out, but we all stepped, you know, back from the trail a few feet and watched them drag him out and cuff him. Hoo boy, was he scroungy-looking! Dirty, scraggly hair all over his head. And hollow cheeks like he hadn't had a good meal in days."

"Which he probably hadn't," I pointed out.

"Yep. And I don't think Lauren is going to want that shirt back. One of the kids crawled into the hole and pulled out her bath towel, too. She's not going to want that either. And there's your stolen sodas."

I looked again at the six-pack, and saw only one was missing. "The guys starving and he only drinks one soda?" I said.

Helen raised an eyebrow. "Well, Estela, they are generic ginger ale. Guess he tried one."

"Humph!" I've never claimed to have discerning taste when it comes to soda, but my ginger ales always tasted okay to me. "What about Diego's sweat pants?"

"I didn't really notice those, but probably. Come to think of it, I think he might have been wearing sweat pants. He wasn't in those orange coverall things the prisoners wear. Good news, though!"

"What's that?"

"Turns out there's a reward for that dude's capture, and we get it! Well, I mean the homeowners here in Arroyo Loco get it. We can buy Diego some new sweat pants and replace Lauren's things. No one's too sure who has to pay to have those mailboxes repaired, but the deputy said even if we had to pay for that, there might be enough left over to throw a party.

They're all still at the roadhouse trying to decide how to spend the money, and getting a good look at that guy locked in the sheriff's SUV. The cops still have the road blocked off."

"Wow. You're right, that is good news. And I'm happy to have our run of bad luck coming to an end. Everyone can come home, and we can feel safe again. And the money, that's good news, too."

"Yeah, except Ernie can pay his own darn hospital bills." Helen snorted and shook her head.

"Why's that, Helen?"

"Well, for one thing, didn't you see? Bryce told the deputies where to look, and they found all of your stuff stashed in that crawl space under their house. Your television, everything. Ernie was trying to freak us all out so we'd finally agree to install cameras all along the road, and put a gate near the highway. Although stealing stuff from you, possibly he was just pissed off at you. Anyway, even now, Bryce says we should use the reward money to put in a security system."

Hoo boy, was right. To be honest, I was a little bit disappointed. I'd already checked with my insurance agent and been assured the insurance company would replace everything that had been stolen with new stuff. Probably now I'd be stuck with my old junk. At least I knew how to work all that old stuff, so there's your silver-lining.

Also, I made a promise to myself on the spot that I would not get caught up in any discussions about what to do with the reward money, although personally, paying off the loans we'd had to take out to cover the cost of the new bridge and street improvements seemed like a better idea than a party.

Helen caught my pensive gaze. "Come on and join us. Nobody's in the mood to make food, and we can't get out to town anyway with all those law enforcement vehicles blocking the road, but folks are talking about ordering in a bunch of pizzas delivered to the roadhouse. This is something to celebrate!"

I had to agree with Helen. On the other hand, my porch felt especially cozy this late afternoon, and I was reluctant to leave. Diego and Alex would be home soon, and with any luck they would be bringing something yummy for dinner.

"Hey, who's that?" Helen squinted, peering down the hill. "That's your godson Diego and Alex, but who is that with them? They must have had to leave their car at the roadhouse."

I craned to see over Helen's shoulder. Three people were walking along the sidewalk toward my house, Diego, Alex, and a woman I didn't recognize. Or maybe I did recognize her. It was hard to judge age at this distance, but she appeared to be in her mid- to late-thirties. Dark curly hair, shorter than Alex, cafe au lait skin and dark eyes.

"You know what, 'Stel'? She looks just like you! Do you know who she is?"

"Maybe." Quietly, I added, "Except I think the last time I saw her, she weighed about seven pounds and was bundled up like a burrito."

Dear Reader

Thank you for reading All Tied Up. I hope you enjoyed it, as well as all of the other books in the Estela Nogales Mystery series and the free short story. I appreciate your support!

Please consider posting reviews for these books on your favorite book-related website. If you liked this story, your friends would probably enjoy hearing about it. I am most grateful for any help in spreading the word.

To keep up on the news about Arroyo Loco, learn about up-coming new releases, and leave me comments and questions, please subscribe to the News at www.cherie.oboyle.com I would love to hear from you!

Sincerely,
Cherie O'Boyle

Thank you!
Thank you to Irene Czech who taught me everything I ever
wanted to know about tarantulas, and a good deal more than
that. Thank you to the burglars who cleaned me out a few
years ago, giving me lots of expertise into that part of the story.
Thank you to Sara McKinley who, in addition to reading these
books and writing glowing reviews, also taught Shiner, Sky, and
me about scent work. And thank you to everyone else who has
crossed my path and left bits and pieces of knowledge and
humor to enliven and populate these pages.

73736927R00145

Made in the USA
Columbia, SC
06 September 2019